ANGEL CITY

ANGEL CITY

Patrick Smith

Pineapple Press, Inc.
Sarasota, Florida

Inquiries should be addressed to:

Pineapple Press, Inc.
P.O. Box 3889
Sarasota, Florida 34230

www.pineapplepress.com

Library of Congress Cataloging-in-Publication Data

Smith, Patrick D., 1927-
  Angel City / Patrick Smith.
     p. cm.
  ISBN 978-1-56164-567-1 (pbk. : alk. paper)
  1. Forced labor--Florida--Fiction. I. Title.
  PS3569.M53785A85 2012
  813'.54--dc23
                            2012026334

ISBN 978-0-910923-64-4 (hardback)
ISBN 978-1-56164-541-1 (e-book)

First Edition
10 9 8 7 6 5 4 3 2 1

Printed in the United States of America

ANGEL CITY

ONE

THERE WAS an unusual chill in the mountain air for late September, but winter comes early in West Virginia, especially on Teeter Ridge. The late afternoon sun was filtered by a swirl of low-hanging clouds, causing the tops of ridges to glow with a somber yellow. The unpainted clapboard house clinging to the side of a hill looked forlorn and foreboding, as if dreading that its aged timbers would once again be drenched with chilling rain.

Jared Teeter stood on the front porch, gazing at the unplowed fields in the valley below, paying no notice to the excited voices inside the house. He left the porch and walked out to the barn with its empty chicken coops and silent stalls — stalls also now empty but still smelling of fresh manure and hot milk. A rat scurrying through a pile of hay in the loft caught his attention momentarily, and he listened intensely, as if expecting the sagging structure to come alive with sounds; then he turned and walked back to the porch. Far in the distance he could see a pickup truck winding its way slowly up the mountain road. He called through the screen door, "Cloma, I think they're beginnin' to come."

An answer came back, "You best feed the hogs now. There won't be time after everyone gets here."

He smiled, saying to himself, "She's as confused as I am. She knows darn well that the hawg pen's been empty now fer more than two weeks."

But just to be sure that it really was empty, he left the porch again and walked toward the fenced plot of barren ground.

Jared Teeter had been born in 1932 in this wooden frame house surrounded by a hundred and sixty acres of West Virginia soil which had been known for almost a century as Teeter Ridge. He was the only one of three Teeter sons to stay behind and live on the land. Both of the other brothers had left home before they reached age twenty, one supposedly going to Baltimore and the other to Chicago. Neither ever returned. Following the death of his father in 1950 and his mother one year later, Jared had lived in the house alone until he married Cloma when he was twenty-three and she sixteen. Their two children, Kristy, the oldest at sixteen, and Bennie, two years younger, were also born in this house. Cloma was now pregnant with a third child.

For several years after it became apparent that he would someday have to leave, Jared clung stubbornly to the land; but each year the tax bills and the cost of clothing and food and gasoline and farm supplies pushed him deeper and deeper into debt. When he finally sold the sturdy old house and the land and paid all the back taxes and the mortgage and the bills, he had only six hundred dollars in cash to show for his lifetime of trying and struggling and finally being forced to admit the stinging reality of defeat. With this money he would have to seek out and build a new life for himself and his family, and he had chosen to do this in Florida.

When the final realization came to Jared, and he had signed the deed to the land, he did not tell Cloma or the children for more than two weeks. They suspected something unusual was happening when Jared sold the milk cow and the hogs and chickens and then his old Cub tractor. Then one day he left in the pickup truck and returned with a 1960 Dodge van, a useless vehicle for a farm. At this moment Cloma knew, but she too remained silent in front of the children.

Jared told them one night at the supper table, and the news was more than they could at once comprehend. Neither Kristy nor Bennie had ever been further away from the farm than an occasional trip into Charleston, and to them this land and the school and church in nearby Dink was all of the world that existed. At first there was a lot of crying. Deep gloom enveloped them, but eventually they accepted the inevitable. And then both of them were pervaded with the excitement of soon seeing a part of the world that had, until then, been only make-believe.

This was the last day for the Teeter family to remain on Teeter Ridge, and that night all the friends from neighboring farms would come to pay their respects.

Jared walked back into the house and to the bedroom, where Cloma was packing the last of their clothes. She looked up at him and said hopefully, "Jay, the bed . . . can't we at least take the bed?"

He had anticipated she would ask this, and had dreaded the moment. He knew what the old brass bed meant to her. It had been his wedding present to her, and in this bed both Kristy and Bennie had been conceived and born; and now another child was within her as a reminder of what this bed meant to their lives together. She had expected that this new child would also be born here. Finally he turned his eyes from her and said softly, "No, Cloma. I'm sorry. There won't be room in the van. I'll get you another brass bed as soon as we're settled."

"It won't be the same," she said. "You know it won't be the same."

"I'm sorry," he said again. Then he turned and walked back to the front porch.

Again Jared watched as the pickup truck groaned up the last few feet of road and turned into the yard. Cloma's mother and father got out and walked to the house. The man was tall and lanky like Jared, but his hair was silver-white and the skin beneath his eyes was deeply marked with chicken tracks caused by too many years of squinting into the sun while following a plow. The woman also had a wrinkled face, but her body was rotund, and she wobbled as she walked.

Jared extended his hand and said, "Howdy. Come on in the house."

The woman greeted him warmly and then went into the house. The man shook hands and remained outside with Jared. He said, "We come a mite early so's I could bring you this. It's fer the trip."

Jared looked at the bills as the old man took them from his coat pocket. He said quickly, "No. I thank you greatly, but I don't need money. We have enough. But I do rightly thank you."

"Take it," the old man insisted. "It's only fifty dollars. We want you to have it as a gift — for the new baby when it comes."

"No," Jared said firmly. "You need it more'n we do."

Cloma's father knew it was useless. He put the bills back into his pocket, suspecting that Jared really needed the money but also knowing what was meant by mountain pride. He said, "Well, if you have need of us in the future, you just write and let us know. We ain't got much, but what we got we'll share."

"I appreciate that," Jared replied, wanting to drop the subject and say nothing more about the money. "Can you smell a storm comin'?" he asked.

"Yes. I smelled it all the way up the mountain. It's goin' to be a humdinger, too. You can bet on that."

Just then two more pickups and an old Chevrolet coupe pulled into the yard. These were followed almost immediately by two more trucks. As each vehicle arrived, the occupants came onto the porch and were greeted by Jared. The women then went inside to present gifts to Cloma of handmade aprons and pot-holders and baby clothes.

The men segregated themselves on the porch while the younger people and children chased each other around the house and through the yard. Conversation on the porch was lively: "We shore hates to see you go, Jay. Maybe you could stay yet and make it o.k."

"Ain't no way," Jared replied. "Use to be a man could make it on a farm just by growin' enough to feed his family and havin' enough left over to get stuff such as flour and salt and shoes. 'Tain't true no more. Now the taxes and the machines and the gasoline and the stuff at the store takes ten times what a fellow can make. The eggs ain't worth the price of chicken feed, and the milk ain't worth the cow feed. Just ain't no way anymore fer a poor man to make it here."

"That's the God's truth!" one man agreed. "Hit's got sometimes where I think I'm goin' to have to et the slop rather than feed it to the hawgs. Them hawgs can always run in the woods and dig out snakes and acorns, but a man ain't a mind to do that."

"Don't know what none of us is goin' to do if'n things don't change soon," another said.

"How fer down in Floridy you plan to go, Jay?" one man asked.

"A fer piece," Jared replied.

"You remember last year, ole Jim Bigley had to sell out

too and leave? He went down to Jacksonville. We got a letter from him sayin' he found work there in a shipyard. Maybe you could stop in Jacksonville and get work with ole Jim."

"Nope," Jared said. "I'll not stop in Jacksonville. So long as we're goin' to Floridy, I want to be where everything is covered with palm trees and oranges. Jacksonville would be 'bout the same as Georgie. I'll go as fer south as a man can go, slam down past Miami, to Homestead. I done looked it up on a map."

"That's a mighty fer piece, all right. But maybe we can all come down and spend Christmas with you. I hear they's a heap to see on one of them Floridy beaches in the winter."

One man laughed and said, "That's probably why ole Jay wants to go so fer down there, so's he can sit around all day and stare at them half-nekked women on the beaches. I've seen pictures of them beaches afore."

Jared said, "Well, you're all welcome to come and stay with us at Christmas time if you've a mind to. We'll be settled by then, and you'll be most welcome. And maybe we can leave the womenfolk at home fer awhile and sneak off to the beach."

"You better shet that up for now," another man said. "Here comes Preacher Will and his missus into the yard. You know he ain't goin' to want to talk about no nekked women runnin' around on a beach."

"He might surprise you," another said, laughing. " 'Specially if they's vittles on that beach."

Kristy and Jeff Billings left the others in the front yard and walked to the fence by the abandoned hog pen. Jeff was one year older than Kristy, and they had been "promised" for the past year since Jeff had carved JEFF + KRISTY on the "promising tree" adjacent to the school in Dink. The old hickory was scarred with dozens and dozens of such inscriptions. Many of the inscribers later became lifemates while others eventually went their separate ways.

Jeff and Kristy's courtship had progressed according to normal mountain customs: passing notes in class, carrying books after school, sitting next to each other in church, long walks on Sunday afternoons, and slipping out of the Saturday night barn dance in order to hold hands and to dare one kiss that would send both of them into violent spells of dizziness.

Kristy was sad that she was going to leave Jeff, but she was too young and too filled with the excitement of life to constantly grieve over it. Jeff wanted to grieve, but instead he pretended that he didn't have that much interest one way or another. On this last night, both of them felt like throwing away their masks and pouring out their inner feelings, but the mountain urge to be above such emotion was prevailing.

Jeff finally broke the silence and said, "I don't care nothin' at all about movin' to Floridy. The mountains is good enough for me."

Kristy thought for a moment, and then she said, "Have you ever seen an orange tree?"

"No. And I don't want to either." Jeff pouted as he said it.

Both said nothing more for a moment, and then Kristy said, "Jeff, I really don't want to move away either. I cried about it for a long time, but I'll not cry any more. I don't really care about orange trees either. What I want someday is an old house just like this one here in the mountains, and a garden to grow things, and a stove to cook meals on, and a brass bed just like Mamma's, and babies . . . lots of babies . . . your babies, Jeff . . . that's what I want most of all. . . ."

Her face flushed as she said it, and Jeff could smell the sweetness of her reddened flesh as she brushed lightly against him. She took his hand in hers and said, "I'll miss you and the mountains, Jeff, but mostly I'll miss you."

Her words rushed through his mind like a mountain wind. He wanted to reach out and hold her close to him forever, but he restrained his emotions and said, "Will you write to me when you get to Floridy? I'll write you back, and then maybe I can come visit you when school ends and the spring plowin' is done."

"I'll write as soon as I can," Kristy promised. "And you better write back right away, you hear?"

Jeff then said, "I brung you a present. I'll go fetch it from the truck, and I'll bring a flashlight so you can see it."

It had now become so dark that Kristy couldn't see Jeff as he turned the side of the house and ran toward the pickup. She was excited by the thought of an unexpected gift, and she wondered what it would be. In a moment Jeff returned and said, "Bet you'll never guess what it is."

Kristy said impatiently, "Jeff, show me! We don't have much time left. They'll be callin' us to supper soon."

Jeff held his hand out and then turned the flashlight on a brightly colored rag doll. He said, "I know you don't play with dolls no more, but my Ma makes the best rag dolls in the mountains, and I had her make this one for you. I remember when you were about six, and we were playin' down by Panther Crick. You got mad and throwed your rag doll into the water, and then you cried somethin' awful as it shot away down the crick and disappeared around a bend. I wanted you to have another one now and take it with you as a reminder of the mountains."

Kristy took the doll and held it against her breasts. "I didn't think you could remember something that happened so long ago," she said. "And I do love this one. I'll keep it always."

"It ain't much," Jeff said proudly, glad that she liked it, "but my Ma made it, and I wanted you to have it. She wanted you to have it too."

"Could you turn off that light now?" Kristy asked.

"Yes. I just wanted you to see the doll."

As soon as the light clicked off, Jeff felt Kristy press against him. He also felt the coming of a violent dizziness.

Preacher Will was the only man present who sported a huge stomach and a fat face. His black wool suit also contrasted with the other men's faded overalls, dungaree pants, khaki pants, and denim windbreakers. For several minutes he stared intensely at the table laden with fried chicken, sliced ham, fried squirrels, venison roast, sweet potato pies, and corn pone. He seemed to be having a hard time restraining himself, and then he said loudly, "May I have yore attention, please?"

All the men came in from the porch, and the women became silent. The preacher said, "For the time bein', leave all them youngens out in the yard. It's time for grownups to have vittles, but afore we eat all this good food the ladies has brought, I best turn up thanks. And I can tell that some of you sinners needs blessin' too afore you gets into them jugs of corn likker I know you got in the trucks. So bow yore heads, please, and cut out that snickerin' afore the Lord sends down a thunderbolt amongst you."

As soon as all became silent again, the preacher said, "Lord, bless this food on this special day, but more 'specially bless the family of Jay Teeter as they depart from amongst us and seek a new life in strange places. Be with them as they search the way, Lord, and see to it they find the kind of home that all God's chillun deserve. They's good folks, Lord, and we'll all miss 'em mightedly, and we ask that You keep 'em in Yore hands and help 'em find the happiness they now seek. Bless us all, oh Lord, and watch over these mountains and all God's chillun. Amen, and let's eat."

Jared said quickly, "Thanks, Brother Will. We appreciate those words. But before everyone starts eatin' I got a few words to say too. When we leave in the mornin' we're not takin' anything in the house with us. They just ain't no room in the van. So I want all of you to come back here in the mornin' and take out what you want. Everything stays behind."

One man said, "That ain't right, Jay. We could sell all this stuff fer you and then send you the money. I'd buy some myself."

"Won't sell a piece of it," Jared said firmly. "All of you know that my Papa built this house afore the turn of the century, and most of this stuff has been in the house since then. Some of it he made hisself. I couldn't sell one piece of it, and I won't rest easy unless I know it's all in the hands of friends."

Cloma spoke up and said, "Don't nobody take the brass bed, though, if you get here afore Papa. Papa has said he'll take it to his place and store it for me, and then we can send for it when we get settled. Everything goes but the brass bed."

Jared was relieved to hear this and was glad that the bed would be safe with Cloma's father. He said, "I'll leave the house open in the mornin', and you can all come back and clean it out. Whatever you don't take will just be wasted with the real estate man, so take it all. Let's eat now, and then we'll have a little fiddle music and some stompin' before everyone goes."

No one needed a second invitation to fill their plates, but no one was as fast as the preacher in reaching the table.

Jared stood on the porch and watched as the last truck headlight disappeared around a bend in the road far below. He sensed that he might have seen the last of his friends for a long time to come, perhaps even forever. He turned and went into the house and said to Bennie, "You best go outside and fetch Skip in, and see to it he stays inside. We'll be leavin' afore dawn, and we won't have time to be chasin' a dog all over the woods."

"Yes, Papa," Bennie said, scrambling for the door.

Jared then took a kerosene lantern from the kitchen shelf, lit it, and turned to Cloma. "I'll be gone fer a bit, but it won't be too long."

She understood what he must do. She said, "You want that I go with you?"

"No. 'Tain't no use fer you to be out in the dark and the night air. I'll go alone."

A dome of orange light sprang outward as he went down the back steps and across the yard. He walked rapidly as he followed a narrow trail that turned north from the barn and ran along the edge of the ridge. Soon he entered a thick growth of hickory trees. The flickering light revealed two granite tombstones in a little clearing which was surrounded by a rusted cast-iron fence. He opened the gate and went inside.

He set the lantern on the ground and dropped to his knees in front of the graves. A glass vase holding faded plastic flowers sat between the two stones. Jared remained silent, thinking of those two times in the past when he had taken a shovel in his hands and physically dug the holes where the two bodies now lay. He had always assumed that he too would someday lie in this plot of ground, but now it seemed that this would never be, and he was afraid.

He also thought of his lifetime on this land, of how deeply his roots were sunk into the West Virginia mountain soil, and the thought of tearing them up so late in life was like ripping out his very heart. For weeks he had been consumed with doubts and anxiety, with a fear of leaving all that he knew and facing the unknown; but he had kept it all hidden within himself as best he could. He did not want Cloma and the children to see his true feelings, for he knew that he must show strength for all of them.

Finally he broke his thoughts and said, "I'm sorry, Papa ... and Mamma ... I done the best I could, but it weren't enough. I just couldn't make it no more ... I tried, but it just couldn't be done. I purely hate to go off and leave you here alone, and I never thought I would. But they ain't nothin' more I can do. I've made sure nobody will ever put plow or axe to this grove and disturb you. It's in the deed, writ right in there, so you can rest easy on that score. Maybe some day we can buy back the land and be with you again. I promise you I'll do my best, I'll try; but now we gotta go. The Lord be with you ... Papa and Mamma ... the Lord be with you. And rest well."

He then got to his feet quickly and walked back along the trail, not looking back again at the grove of darkened hickory trees.

When he approached the house, all was in darkness except for a dim glow coming from behind a drawn window shade in his and Cloma's bedroom. Sharp rumbles of thunder were rushing in from the west, signalling the coming of a storm. Brilliant fingers of lightning shot downward and disappeared into the black outlines of distant ridges. For a moment Jared watched as the lightning moved eastward, and then he opened the back door as quietly as possible and walked softly down the hall to the bedroom.

Cloma was in the bed asleep, so Jared tried to make no sound as he removed his clothes. He looked at Cloma's tousled blonde hair and marveled at how much Kristy looked like her. Both had the same blonde hair, delicate nose and cheekbones, and thin mouth. Bennie was just the opposite, with Jared's black hair, full face, and the tall lanky body of a mountain man. Although tall, Bennie still had the look of a boy, but Kristy — like most mountain girls her age — already had the fully developed body of a woman, a mountain child-woman. Jared had always said that both he and Cloma had been allowed to stamp one child each from their own individual molds. When Cloma had become pregnant again, Jared teased her that now they would have a sandy-haired boy who would have the features of both of them.

Suddenly Cloma said sleepily, "Is that you, Jay?" Then she pushed herself up and said, "The youngens was dog-tired from all the excitement of the day. They went on to bed right after Bennie caught Skip and brung him inside. I hope you didn't have much for them to do tonight."

"No, there wasn't nothin' more to do. It's best they went on to bed. We got a long way to travel."

He turned off the light and slipped under the covers beside her, putting his hand across her swollen stomach. It seemed to him that every little thing that he did now reminded him of something in the past. As he was immersed in darkness he thought of how proud he had been that day several years ago when he finally ran the electric line to the house. All of them had stayed up half the night clicking the lights off and on, like children with new toys on Christmas morning.

Cloma pushed herself closer to Jared and said, "I'm afraid, Jay. Maybe I shouldn't be, but I am."

"Afraid of what, the storm?" he asked.

"No. Not that. I'm afraid of what lies ahead for all of us."

"You got nothin' to fret about," Jared said reassuringly as he moved his hand back and forth across her stomach. "We'll make it fine . . . I promise you. The Lord will look after us. What I'm worried about most is you and that little fellow inside you. You sure you feel up to leavin' now? We could move around and stay with different folks 'til the baby comes."

"I feel fine, and I'd rather go now. That way we could be settled sommers when the baby comes. It'd be easier to go now than wait 'til later."

"All right. We'll go on and go as we planned. But if you get to feelin' poorly along the way, you best let me know. We'll stop sommers and stay put 'til you feel like movin' on again."

Cloma did not answer, and Jared could feel that she had already drifted back to sleep. He held her gently and said softly, "Don't you fret none, Cloma. We'll make out fine. You'll see."

For several minutes Jared listened as the storm moved closer to Teeter Ridge. He knew that soon now it would lash his land with its full fury. He was concerned about the hogs and the chickens and the cow until he realized that they were no longer there. He suddenly sprang upright in the bed as if a bolt of lightning had crashed through the roof and seared into his body. A cold fear of what lay ahead swept through his veins and caused sweat to form on his brow. He tried to calm himself but the flashes of lightning and the booming thunder made the apprehension worse. His hands trembled as he tried to push himself back under the covers.

Cloma came awake and said to him, "What's the matter, Jay? You're jumpin' around like a new colt."

" 'Tain't nothin' but the storm. It sounded like the lightnin' hit awful close by. I'm sorry I woke you again, so just go on back to sleep now."

Again he put his arms around her, this time trying vainly to shut away all consciousness of the storm and to dispel from himself the pent-up spectre of disaster that had finally erupted from every pore of his body.

TWO

THE HOOD of the old Dodge van seemed to be sweating as the vehicle chugged unsteadily along Highway 27, passing a line of Australian pines on the left and an open field on the right. The mid-day Florida sun was sending waves of heat shimmering upward from the cracked concrete. The van suddenly shuddered and belched forth a hissing cloud of angry steam. Valves clanked and rattled as the truck rolled slowly to a stop beside a drainage canal flanking the right side of the highway.

Jared got out of the van and raised the hood. When he removed the radiator cap he released a violent geyser of boiling water. He jumped back, shook his scorched hand and muttered, "Jesus!"

For a moment he stared at the hissing radiator, then he walked to the side of the van and said, "It'll take that thing a while to cool down afore I can put in some water. We might as well eat now."

Cloma pulled herself slowly from the right door of the van. Her stomach seemed more swollen than ever. She was followed by Kristy and Bennie.

Cloma settled herself unsteadily on the ground and spread out a newspaper. From a brown paper bag she removed four cans of Vienna sausage, a box of crackers, and four bottles of hot Coke. They all sat in the white limestone dust and started eating silently.

Jared looked past the drainage canal and across the field that stretched as far as the eye could see toward the horizon. Far in the distance, giant sheets of water were being sprayed into the air, and a group of people followed a truck piled high with crates. Jared took a bite of the sausage and said, 'I ain't never seen a field like that in my lifetime. It looks like the whole world out there, don't it?"

Cloma looked but said nothing.

Bennie said, "Can I let Skip out of the truck, Papa? He probably needs to do his job."

"No. You better not. He might run out in the highway and get himself killed. You better leave him in the van 'til we get there."

"How much farther is it, Papa?" Kristy asked.

" 'Tain't far now. We're almost to Homestead. We'll be there in just a little bit more, and then we can all rest up some."

"I want to see the ocean," Bennie said, excitement in his voice. "You said that when we got to Floridy we would see the ocean, and we ain't seen it yet."

"It's over in the east," Jared said. "You'll get to see it soon enough."

"Will we get to fish in the ocean?" Bennie asked.

"Yes. We'll fish. And someday we might even own our own boat."

"I don't want to catch any smelly ole fish," Kristy said tartly. "I want a bathin' suit. A red one in two pieces, just like you see in the magazines."

"You all better worry about where we'll sleep tonight,

and forget all that foolishness for now," Cloma said wearily
as she gathered up the empty cans.

"Are you feelin' all right, Cloma?" Jared asked.

"Yes. I'm fine. I'm just fine."

"Are you sure?"

"Yes, Jay, I'm fine!" she insisted. "I'm just fine."

"Well, if you get to feelin' poorly again, we'll try to find
a motel."

"We can't afford a motel," Cloma said firmly. "And I've
already said I'm feelin' fine. That spell the other day was just
an upset stomach. I'm fine now."

Jared went to the van and came back with a bucket. He
filled it in the drainage canal and took the water back to the
van. Cloma gathered up the newspapers and bottles and put
them back into the brown paper bag.

When Jared cranked the engine, they all got back inside,
and the van pulled slowly back onto the highway and headed
south.

The Teeter family had been on the road for almost two
weeks on a trip they had expected to take no more than four
or five days. The morning they left the West Virginia farm
before daylight, they had all been drenched by a bone-
chilling rainstorm, and the dog Skip had managed to jump
from the van and escape into the darkness. Bennie had chased
him for a half-hour before hemming him up in the barn and
returning him soaking wet to the van.

Misfortune plagued them almost constantly. When Jared
traded his pickup truck for the Dodge van, he had taken the
word of the salesman that the van was in good condition.
Before they reached the West Virginia state line, the water-
pump gave out and had to be replaced, causing them the loss
of the better part of a day. A universal joint stripped itself in
North Carolina, and then the next day two tires blew out and

shredded. They spent three days in a small town in north
Georgia waiting at a garage for a new generator to be shipped
in from Atlanta, a generator that all the while had been on a
shelf in the rear of the garage but was now priced higher because of "shipping charges." One night they stayed in a motel,
but the rest of the nights they slept in the van. Then it was
the spark plug wires and a coil, and finally the radiator became hostile as they moved deeper into warm weather. This
slowed them to below the legal speed limit. Just north of
Jacksonville, Jared was arrested and fined thirty-five dollars
for a faulty brake light. The court appearance and the repairs
took another day. Jared's limited supply of cash had
diminished quickly in a series of roadside garages and unexpected delays. And then to avoid any more fines on the
heavily-policed interstate highways, Jared drove inland and
traveled along less used state roads leading south to Lake
Okeechobee and then Homestead.

All of this did not dampen the excitement of Kristy and
Bennie, but it brought even deeper anxiety to Jared and
Cloma. To the youngsters the trip had turned into an adventure; but to Jared and Cloma it was still the end of all things
they had ever known.

With each mile they traveled, Jared's emotions ran up and
down like a yo-yo. One moment he was optimistic and confident, and the next moment he was cast again into deep doubt.
He tried to appear cheerful and confident, but Cloma knew
that he was tormented with doubt.

Kristy and Bennie stared out of the window in the rear
door of the van as they approached the outskirts of Homestead. They had both been fascinated since they first entered
the citrus country to the north of Lake Okeechobee. The
miles and miles of trees laden with golden fruit seemed to
them to be all the Christmases they had known rolled into

one, since the only time they had ever seen or eaten oranges was on Christmas morning when they found them under the sparsely decorated tree.

On both sides of the highway there were now vegetable fields intermingled with groves of avocado and papaya and mangoes and limes and other strange things they had never seen. Farm roads leading off to the left and right were lined with towering Australian pines and stately royal palms and dumpy cabbage palms. Stands displaying an endless variety of fruits and vegetables were located at almost every intersection.

Jared suddenly turned to Cloma and said, as if in an unexpected revelation, "That's what we'll have, Cloma! A roadside stand where we can sell fruits and vegetables. We'll do it as soon as we can save up the money. We can make ourselves a good livin' with a stand. It won't take us no time at all to get one."

Cloma considered the idea for a moment, and then she said enthusiastically, "That would be real good. Maybe we could make some things ourselves and sell them too. You were always good at makin' cane-bottom chairs, and Kristy makes real fine pot-holders. Bennie could make whatnot shelves and those little carved animals he makes, and I could sew aprons and blouses and make those red and yellow sunbonnets some folks like. If we had a little piece of land behind the stand, we could grow our own vegetables too."

Jared was pleased that she agreed. He smiled as he said with his first excitement in weeks, "We'll do it! It won't take us no time at all!"

The two-lane highway was now jammed with huge trucks and cars and pickups, all seemingly frantic to move faster toward a distant destination. Driving became more and more difficult for Jared, and the task took all of his attention. He prayed silently that the radiator would not boil again and force him from the highway.

Highway 27 was also the main street leading through the business section of Homestead, and Jared felt a tremendous sensation of relief when he passed the city limits of this place they had searched for so long and had endured so many difficulties to reach. He sighed when he stopped for the first traffic light. But his feeling of relief that the long trip was finally ended was immediately replaced by the bewilderment of being in a totally strange place and not knowing where to go or what to do. He drove the van even more slowly, backing up traffic behind him and causing other impatient drivers to honk their horns and gesture angrily. They all stared like tourists as they passed block after block of stores and restaurants and cocktail lounges and supermarkets unlike anything they had ever seen in their rural section of West Virginia.

On the southern end of the city they came to an area of huge packing houses where the vegetables were processed before being shipped to distant markets. Before he realized it, Jared had left Homestead and entered Florida City. He finally pulled to the side of the road and stopped.

For a moment they all became silent with exhaustion, and then Bennie said, "I gotta leak, Papa. And I know Skip is about to bust."

The small black and white dog was leaning against one wall of the van, panting.

Cloma said, "We should have never brought that dog with us. We could have given him away. A trip like this is no place for a dog."

"Aw, Cloma, you know the kids couldn't leave Skip behind," Jared said. "And besides, he won't be any trouble."

Bennie put his arm around the dog and said, "I'll take care of him, Mamma. You don't need to worry none about him."

"I'll find a service station and get gas, and you can use the restrooms there," Jared said, cranking the motor again.

He pulled into a station on the next corner. Bennie took

Skip behind the building while his mother and Kristy went to the women's room.

The attendant set the automatic control on the pump nozzle and said to Jared, "You folks tourists?"

"No," Jared said. "We're down here lookin' for work."

"You mean picking?" the man asked.

"Well, anything," Jared replied. "I'm not particular just so long as it's honest work."

"Jobs in the fields are pretty hard to come by right now, and that's about all there is around here," the man said as he stared at Jared's lanky body and faded overalls. "Besides all the regular migrants, the place is swarming with Cubans, and there's been a steady stream of folks like you coming in here from the Carolinas and West Virginia and Georgia and Alabama and all over the place. I ain't never seen nothing like it."

"You mean there ain't no work?" Jared asked, deep concern in his voice.

"Well, there's some, but you sure got to look to find it. And it might be pretty hard for you with no experience. There's a line-up every morning right over yonder on the street corner."

"What's that?" Jared asked.

"All the folks who want jobs in the field gather over there, and the contractors hire who they want. If you want to try that, you better get there early, way before sun-up. There's always a lot more people than jobs."

"I'll be there," Jared said.

The man then turned his attention from Jared and watched Kristy as she came from the restroom and walked back to the van. He noticed every move of her body, the full breasts and hips, and then he said to Jared, "That your girl?"

"That's my daughter Kristy," Jared replied.

"How old is she?"

"She's sixteen, and she's a mighty fine girl," Jared said proudly.

The man studied Kristy closely again, and then he said, "The way she's built, she could easily pass for twenty. She could get a job real easy."

"How's that?" Jared asked curiously.

"Can she dance?"

"Back home we had a barn dance every Saturday night. She's pretty good at it."

"I mean go-go dance," the man said. "She could get a job easy in any of the lounges, and that pays good money. She could get you by 'til you find work."

"What's this go-go dancin'?" Jared asked.

The man looked at Jared curiously and said, "You know, fellow, go-go. Dancing naked from the waist up with the tits showing. The way she's built, she could take her pick of the joints."

An instant rage boiled up within Jared. He said quickly, "How much I owe you, fellow?"

"Eight dollars even. You want the oil checked?"

"I don't want nothin' more from you!" Jared shot back angrily. His hands trembled as he handed the man the money. Then he jumped into the van and screeched the tires as he drove away.

Cloma was startled by the sudden burst of speed. She said, "What's the matter, Jay? Did somethin' happen back there?"

"No. Nothin'," Jared said, trying to calm his voice. "It's gettin' late, and we gotta try and find a place to make camp fer tonight."

Jared turned the van back east, and then he drove slowly along a narrow side street. It took him several minutes to brush from his mind the thought of Kristy dancing naked in a bar. He knew he had come close to striking the man but was glad that he had simply driven away. Trouble was one thing he did not need at this point.

He soon came to a small park with swings, benches and a picnic area with a covered pavilion and barbeque grille. No one was there, so Jared turned the van into the park and stopped by the pavilion. He said, "This looks about as good as we'll find. And there's a roof fer me and Bennie to sleep under while you and Kristy can have the van."

Bennie said, "Can I let Skip out of the truck, Papa?"

"Well, you better put a rope around his neck and tie him to the front bumper. They's bound to be rabbits around here, and I don't feel a mind to be chasin' Skip all over south Floridy."

Jared took two bedrolls out of the van and placed them on the concrete beneath the pavilion. He turned to Cloma and said, "How much vittles we got left?"

Cloma settled herself on a bench and replied, "We got about a half-dozen cans of Vienna sausage, some bread, and a can of peaches."

"That'll do fer tonight," Jared said. "I'll see to some supplies in the mornin'."

Bennie came running around the side of the van and said with excitement, "They's a bunch of funny-lookin' trees right over yonder, Papa! And they got real bananas growin' on them! You want me to go and pick some for supper?"

"No. You better not do that. They probably belong to somebody. But you better scout around and scrape up some branches. We'll need a fire later."

Kristy came from the van and said, "Papa, they's somethin' bitin' all over me. It stings somethin' awful."

Jared suddenly slapped at his face and arms and said, "Skeeters! Jesus, the whole place is swarmin' with skeeters. That's all we need now, to be et alive by skeeters. Maybe we can smoke 'em away."

Bennie slapped his arms and said, "I'll get the wood now, Papa. We'll show them skeeters a thing or two for sure."

The sun was just beginning to set when the patrol car

passed the park. The officer inside noticed the West Virginia tag and the bedrolls under the pavilion. He turned, came back and parked beside the van. Then he got out and said, "You folks having a cookout?"

Jared got up from the bench and said, "No, we're not doin' any cookin'. We done et. We're just tryin' to run the skeeters off with the smoke."

The officer was a young man of about thirty. He looked to the van and then back to Jared. "I see you folks are from West Virginia. That's a pretty far piece from here. You just down for a vacation?"

"No, we come to stay," Jared replied. "We just got in this afternoon, and I'll start lookin' fer work tomorrow."

"Well," the officer said hesitantly, "it's o.k. for you to eat here and rest for a while, but you can't stay the night. Overnight camping in a city park is against the law. You'll have to move on before dark."

Jared didn't understand. He said, "Ain't this public property?"

"Yes, it's public property," the officer replied.

"Back in West Virginny, anybody who wants to can camp on public property so long as they don't disturb nothin'. We ain't doin' no harm."

"I'm sorry," the officer said, noticing that the woman was heavy with child. "It's the law, and there's nothing I can do about it. Why don't you go to a motel or a boarding house for the night?"

"I guess we could," Jared said, "but we just can't rightly afford it. We had a lot of bad luck comin' down, and we need to save all the money we can."

"You can go to the Salvation Army place, then," the officer said.

"The Salvation Army?" Jared questioned. "We're mountain folk, and we don't take charity from nobody."

The officer was trying to be patient because of the

woman and the children. Turning migrants out of the park at
night was a regular nightly routine for him. He said, "It
wouldn't exactly be charity. The Salvation Army is there just
to help folks like you when they need help. They have a big
empty lot with trees where you could park the van for tonight and make camp. Just doing that wouldn't be charity."

"I guess we could do that," Jared said. "We do need a
place to camp fer tonight, and as soon as I find work tomorrow, I'll look about and find us a boardin' house 'til we
can get our own place. We don't want to break any laws.
We're peaceable folks. All we want is to make a home here."

The officer was relieved. He said, "Well, you go right up
there one block, turn left, go for four more blocks, and the
Salvation Army is right on the corner. You can't miss it. It's a
big two-story white frame house."

As soon as the patrol car had left, Jared gathered up the
bedrolls and put them into the van. Bennie untied Skip and
brought him inside, and then they drove slowly up the street.
Jared found the house with no trouble, and he parked the
van beneath a huge live oak. He then got out and walked to
the front of the house.

A man got up from a rocking chair on the porch and
came to meet Jared. He looked Jared over carefully and said,
"Something we can do for you?"

Jared still did not like the idea of being here, and he was
glad that his friends back in West Virginia would never know
that he had gone to the Salvation Army. He said reluctantly,
"We just need a place to park the van fer tonight and make
camp. A policeman sent us here. Is it o.k. there under the
tree?"

"That's fine," the man said. "You folks just passing
through?"

"No, we're here to stay," Jared answered. "I'll find work
tomorrow, and then I'll get us a place. We had some bad luck
comin' down."

"If you want, there's empty bunks upstairs. It's free, and you can sleep inside out of the night air. There's also hot showers."

"We'll stay in the van," Jared replied.

"Suit yourself. You can park out there as long as you like. We've got a sitting room inside with a TV. While you're out looking for work tomorrow, your folks can stay here. And supper will be ready in about fifteen minutes. It's nothing fancy — hot franks and beans, cole slaw, and hot coffee. You're welcome to eat with us if you wish."

The thought of hot food and coffee interested Jared. He had not had coffee for more than a week, and he knew that the others were not satisfied with the small cans of Vienna sausage that had been their supper. He said, "How much does it cost?"

"It's free," the man replied.

"We can't take your food fer nothin'," Jared said. "We're mountain folk, and we don't take charity. How much would it cost if we paid?"

The man hesitated for a moment, and then he said, "Well, you can put whatever you wish in the donation box inside the hall. I'd say that fifty cents would be fine for all of you."

"That seems fair enough," Jared said. "We'll all come on inside as soon as we make camp. And we do thank you rightly fer letting us park the van."

"That's what we're here for," the man replied. As he turned and went back up the steps to the porch, he muttered to himself, "Mountain folk!"

THREE

JARED WAS up before dawn the next morning and left the Salvation Army building before breakfast. He drove directly to the street corner where the man at the service station had told him the line-up was held each day. Several pickup trucks and old buses were already parked beneath a street light, and a large group of men and women were milling around silently, waiting for the ritual to begin.

Jared noticed that some of the people were white and some black; some were Cubans and some Mexicans, although he could not tell one from another; and others were long-haired, bearded hippies accompanied by young girls with strings of wooden beads around their necks and sweatbands tied around their foreheads. All of them had expressionless faces and moved about as if in a trance. Each of them — both men and women — somehow resembled the other.

It was but a few minutes when a man stood up in the back of a truck and shouted, "I need twenty-five hands for okra!" People pushed by Jared frantically and formed a line. As soon as the twenty-five were hired and given passes to board a bus, the others in the line moved to another truck.

Jared watched with interest as two more crews were hired. The whole process seemed to him like he had always imagined an ancient slave market to be. He finally realized that unless he fought his way into a line, he would still be standing on the curb when the last bus was filled.

When another man shouted an order for tomato pickers, Jared pushed his way into the crowd and worked his way forward. When he reached the head of the line, the man glanced at him briefly and said, "You got experience picking tomatoes?"

Jared said, "Well, I owned my own farm back in West Virginny, and I growed a few tomatoes. I always picked what I growed."

"Step aside," the man said briskly. "I don't want nothing but experienced pickers. We got a sixty-acre field to clear this morning, and we ain't got time to fool with no friggin' hill-billy."

"But I can do it," Jared insisted. "I owned my own. . ."

"Goddamit, fellow, are you deaf?" the man said impatiently. "Move aside! I ain't got all day to get this bus rolling."

Jared moved out of the line and walked dejectedly back to the curb. He made no other attempt to get into a line as he watched the last bus being loaded. Several dozen other people had also been turned away or had failed to make it to the head of the lines, and they slowly drifted away into the shadows. Jared was alone beneath the street light as dawn streaked through the eastern sky.

For a half-hour Jared sat on the curb, gazing absently at the buses and trucks that ambled by, trying to determine what he must do now. Finally he decided to try the packing houses. He got into the van and drove along the main street into Homestead.

It did not bother him that he had left Cloma and the

children behind while he looked for work, for he knew that watching the TV would be a real treat to them. He had also left the money with Cloma to pay for the meals while he was gone.

When he reached the last packing house on the western outskirts of the city, he stopped and went inside. As soon as he inquired about work, he was told that only experienced graders were needed, and that all other jobs were filled. From one plant he went to another, working his way back toward Florida City; and at each plant the story was the same.

It was mid-morning when he was rejected by the last packing house, and he felt more despondent and hopeless than ever. He then drove the van back into Homestead, parked in a city lot, and started walking the streets. At first the tourists in their shorts and brightly colored shirts and blouses interested him, but then his thoughts went back only to finding a job.

Soon he came to a farm supply store and went inside to inquire about work on the loading platform or driving a truck, but again there was none. He then left the main area of town and walked along a narrow side street lined with dingy pawn shops and bargain stores. Already there were faceless men sitting along the sidewalk, drinking from bottles inside brown paper bags. Jared finally paused when he passed the front of a place called Blue Moon Cafe and noticed a sign in the window that read: "Help Wanted."

Jared went inside reluctantly, almost certain that he would not be suitable for work in a cafe. The small room was dimly lit and smelled strongly of boiled cabbage and stale bacon grease. There was a counter at the back of the room, and tables occupied the center and sides. Except for two men drinking coffee at the counter, the place was empty.

For several moments Jared stood by the counter and shuffled his feet nervously, thinking that perhaps it was a mistake even to come inside. Then a short fat man wearing a dirty apron and a white cap came from the kitchen area and said to him, "What'll it be, fellow?"

"Well," Jared said hesitantly, "I noticed the sign in the window. I'm lookin' fer work, and I just thought I'd come in and ask about it."

The man eyed Jared closely and said, "My dishwasher took sick yesterday and will be out for a couple of days. The pay is a buck an hour, and you can put in seven hours today and thirteen tomorrow. You want it?"

Jared replied quickly, "Yes. I'll do it. When you want me to start?"

"Right now," the man replied. "All them breakfast dishes is piled up back there, and I can't tend to it and cook and wait the tables. Come on back and I'll show you what to do."

Jared followed the man into the kitchen area. On one side there was a stove filled with simmering pots of squash and cabbage and black-eyed peas, and a huge frying pan. Against the opposite wall there were two large sinks, one filled with a combination of greasy water and tired soap suds, and the other plain water.

The man said to Jared, "You wash 'em in here and rinse in there. After you dry 'em, stack 'em on the shelf over yonder. It's also your job to clear the tables and the counter and keep the floor swept. At quitting time, you put out all the slop and garbage. We start serving breakfast at five, so be here a little before that in the morning. And let's get something straight right now, fellow. The pay don't include no meals. What you eat you pay for. And everything you break comes out of your wages. You understand?"

"Yes, I understand," Jared said. He had a sickening feeling as he stared at the huge mound of dirty dishes and utensils stacked on a table beside the sink.

The man turned to leave, and then he looked back at Jared and said, "You better go sommers tonight and take a bath and wash them overalls. The way you look, you'll have the health department down on me."

Jared glanced down briefly at his dirty clothes, and then he grimaced as he picked up a dish and tried to wash the dried egg yolk from it in the greasy water.

It was nearly dark when Jared returned to the Salvation Army building. Cloma, Kristy and Bennie were sitting on a bench beneath the huge oak tree. Jared parked the van, walked over to them and settled himself wearily on the bench.

Cloma said, "We was gettin' real worried about you, Jay. You've been gone so long."

"I tried a little bit of everything," Jared said. "They wouldn't hire me at the line-up because I didn't have no experience, and then I tried all the packin' houses and a few stores. Don't seem to be nothin' around here fer a man to do, so's we might have to move on sommers else. Maybe it would be better up in the cattle country."

Cloma noticed the tiredness in his voice. She said encouragingly, "Maybe it will be better tomorrow. We only been here two days now. Maybe tomorrow you'll find what you want."

"I got work fer tomorrow. And I worked seven hours today. It didn't pay but a dollar an hour, but I guess that's better than nothin'."

Cloma was surprised by this. She asked curiously, "Where'd you work?"

"In a cafe."

"A cafe?" Cloma questioned. "You don't know anything about that kind of work. What'd you do?"

"I worked," Jared said guardedly, wishing that he had not even told them about it.

"Doin' what?" Cloma insisted.

Jared remained silent for a moment, and then he cast his eyes downward and said, "Washin' dishes."

Cloma put her hand on his arm and said, "Jared . . . Jared . . . you didn't have to do that. We're not that hard up yet, are we?"

"It was honest work," he insisted defensively.

Kristy jumped up and said, "Papa, you ought not be washin' dishes in a cafe. I'll wash the dishes tomorrow, and you can look for other work. That's not the kind of thing for you to do."

Jared considered the idea briefly, and then he said, "Would you really do that, Kristy? It would mean thirteen dollars, and I could go on lookin' fer somethin' else. Maybe tomorrow I'll try all the service stations. I sure know how to pump gas and fix flat tires, and somebody is bound to need help."

"I'll do it, Papa!" Kristy said enthusiastically.

For the first time that day, Jared became aware of how hungry he was. He had not eaten since the night before, and now his stomach was rumbling. He said, "Well, it's settled then. I'll look around for another day before we decide what else to do. But right now I sure need to go inside and have some vittles. I'm powerful hongry, and even them franks and beans would go good."

When he got up, Cloma stood by him and took his hand in hers. She said, "Jared, I ain't ashamed of what you did today. I know you did it for all of us. You're a good man, Jared Teeter, and I love you for it. You got no need to be ashamed."

He put his arm around her, and they walked together to the two-story white frame building.

Cloma and Bennie rode with Jared when he took Kristy to the Blue Moon Cafe the next morning. Although it was not yet five, the place was already filled with solemn men dressed as field hands, and the owner was impatient as he told Jared that it was all right for Kristy to substitute for him at the sinks so long as she could keep up with the work. Kristy insisted that she could. Jared paid the man the price of a breakfast and lunch for Kristy, and then he went back to the van and started driving the streets.

Only one service station in Homestead was open at that hour, and the manager had nothing to offer in the way of work. He returned to the Salvation Army, had breakfast with Cloma and Bennie, and then left them behind as he started on his rounds again.

By late morning he had visited every station between Homestead and Florida City, and there were no jobs available. He had given up hope and was ready to quit when he pulled into one last station on the west side of Florida City. He parked behind the building, and walked to the front.

No customers were there, and the manager was standing outside by a pump island. When Jared came to him he said, "Something I can do for you?"

Jared anticipated what the answer would be as he asked, "I'm lookin' fer work, and I thought maybe you needed some help. I can pump gas or fix flats or do 'most anything you want me to do."

The man studied Jared, and then he asked, "Where you from, fellow?"

"West Virginny. We just got down here a couple of days ago."

"How much family you got?"

"I got a girl sixteen and a boy fourteen."

"They good and healthy?"

"Yes," Jared replied, beginning to wonder at the questions that had nothing to do with his request for a job.

"How about your old lady?" the man then asked.

"Well, she's strong, but she's about seven months along with a new baby."

The man looked at Jared closely again and said, "I ain't

got no work here just now, but have you thought about
doing any picking?''

"They wouldn't hire me in that line-up yesterday mornin','' Jared said, disappointed at being turned down again.
"But I would sure do it or anythin' if I could just find work.''

"Well, that line-up don't mean nothing. It's just a one-day
shot for drifters and bums. I'm talking about steady work.
I can probably help you if you want me to.''

"That would be mighty fine of you,'' Jared said quickly,
surprised by the unexpected offer. "I'd sure appreciate anything you can do.''

Jared waited outside as the man went into the station
office, picked up the phone and dialed. In a moment he said,
"This Creedy? . . . yeah . . . this is Hankins at the service station . . . you need some people? . . . no, they're not black,
they're white . . . hillbilly types from West Virginia . . . four
of them . . . not the kind to give you trouble I don't think . . .
man's around forty . . . says he has a strong boy and a girl
. . . the woman's knocked up, though . . . a white Dodge van,
about a '60 or '61 . . . o.k., I'll send them to the regular
place . . . you'll meet them first thing in the morning then
. . . three of them can work, so at twenty bucks a head, you
owe me sixty dollars, and I want the money tonight . . . bring
it to the station around eight.''

The man then hung up the phone and came back out to
Jared. "Well, I've got you folks fixed up with some jobs,'' he
said.

"You really mean it?'' Jared exclaimed, breaking into a
broad grin. "I don't know how to thank you. I was about
ready to give up.''

"Glad to help out. You don't need to thank me. The man
who's going to see you is named Creedy. Silas Creedy. You
can camp tonight in a hammock about four miles down 27.
It's on the left of the road just behind a sign advertising the
Everglades National Park. You can't miss it. He'll meet you

there first thing in the morning. You do a good job, this'll probably be steady work for a long time to come."

"I'll do a good job," Jared said eagerly, "and I sure don't know how to thank you enough." He extended his hand and said, "My name's Teeter. Jared Teeter. Folks call me Jay."

The man shook his hand briefly. "Glad to meet you, Jay." he said.

Jared then handed the man a ten-dollar bill and said, "This is just a little somethin' to say thanks. I really appreciate it."

The man took the bill and put it into his pocket. He said, "Well, o.k., but I didn't expect any money. I was just helping you out, that's all. Folks has to help each other these days."

"That's what I always believed. Folks has to help each other. And I sure thank you plenty."

Jared then got into the van and drove quickly back to the Salvation Army place. He rushed up the steps and found Cloma and Bennie inside the sitting room. He did a brisk jig on the worn wooden floor and said to them, "I told you! I told you comin' down here, didn't I? We're goin' to be o.k. I've got steady work already!"

"Are you foolin' me, Jared?" Cloma asked anxiously.

"No, it's the God's truth! A man at a filling station made a phone call, and somebody named Creedy is goin' to come in the mornin' and give us work. We're to stay tonight in a hammock down south of here. I've got the directions."

"We'll need food," Cloma said with excitement, trying to control the flood of relief this news was bringing to her.

"And ice," Jared said, "a big bag of ice so's we can have cold drinks. We'll pick up Kristy first, then we'll go to a market and get all the things we need fer tonight and in the mornin'. We'll get some candy bars fer the kids, and some sweet buns and fresh fruit, and some meat scraps fer Skip, and. . . ."

"Oh, Jay, I'm so glad," Cloma interrupted. "I was so

afraid for us."

"We're goin't to be just fine," Jared said, reaching over and pressing her hand. "You needin' worry one bit. We'll have our own place afore time fer the baby to come. And we can send fer the bed, too."

FOUR

A BRISK coolness was in the air as a mid-October dawn broke the clear Florida sky. The sun would soon send waves of dry heat across the land as it inched upward in the sky, making the soil a hostile enemy that scorched plants and strained the endurance of a man; but now the ground was covered with millions of glistening moisture jewels that changed color constantly with the growing light.

Jared awoke slowly and gazed upward into the tops of the cabbage palms. The thickness of the trees, combined with the heavy growths of palmetto, filtered the yet weak sunlight and caused the hammock to glow dimly like the coals of a dying fire. For a moment more he lay still, then he bolted upright and jumped to his feet. He calmed himself only when he looked to the left, saw the van, and realized where he was.

He moved quietly so as not to awaken anyone. After gathering sticks and starting a fire, he turned up the dirt trail leading back to the highway. When he reached the edge of the ribbon of black asphalt, he squatted on his haunches and looked out across the fields that melted into the distant horizon. A thin layer of fog lay motionless just above the ground. It was broken into wisps as egrets swooped upward and downward while searching the fields for food.

Jared gazed intensely for several minutes, thinking not of a time here in this strange Florida hammock, but back once again to those acres in West Virginia where the soil was mixed with the blood of his father and his mother and his wife and children. Times there had been hard, and sometimes almost desperate, but he had been his own man in a world of his own making. He had been beholden to no one as he now must be, but the price for this foolish and stubborn pride had been more than he could pay and was now coming up for collection.

He thought of Cloma, lying pregnant on the hard floor of the van, and of the day so long ago when they met at a church social as he bid fifty cents for her box of fried chicken, which he later shared with her. Their meeting had been nothing more than his contribution to the church build-ing fund, or so it seemed at the exact moment; but as they walked to the picnic table by the church to spread the dinner, he accidentally touched her shoulder, and he knew instantly that he would spend his life with her.

He thought again of all those doubts and anxieties that had tormented him during the trip southward from West Virginia, asking himself if he had really done the right thing or if he should have tried for one more year to hold on to the land. But he knew that his situation there had been hopeless and there was no other way except to leave; but the leaving had been an almost unbearable knife thrust through his heart.

It troubled him deeply to take Kristy and Bennie out of school, for the one thing he was determined to do in life was to give them the education which had been denied to him and to Cloma. He had not gone past the tenth grade, and Cloma had dropped out of the eleventh grade when they married. But there would be schools in Florida, and later there would be college, and roads would open for Kristy and Bennie that had been forever closed to him.

He knew that many things he left behind would haunt his memory forever: the woods where he hunted, the streams where he fished, the hillsides where he cut wood to keep them warm in winter, the fields that produced skimpy crops of corn and pumpkins, the barn with its early morning smells, the hickory grove where his father and mother rested; all these things would linger while the hurt and the pain and the hopelessness and the despair would someday fade away. But he was determined to push all of his former life from his mind, and create something new and good for all of them.

His trance was broken when he heard footsteps coming quickly up the dirt trail. He turned as Kristy ran up and said, "Mamma sent me lookin' for you, Papa. She said the coffee is ready."

Jared motioned and said, "Sit here beside me a minute, Kristy."

When she was settled on the damp grass, he said, "I want to thank you again fer what you did fer me in the cafe."

"It was nothing, Papa," she said. "I was just glad to help out."

"We're all going to be fine," Jared said, reaching over and touching her arm. "You'll see. Everything is going to work out o.k."

For a moment Kristy stared across the misty field in silence, and then she said, "Papa . . . I know everything is going to be fine with us . . . but someday . . . when we're all settled and Mamma and Bennie are taken care of . . . I want to go back to the mountains. Papa . . . do you understand?"

"I reckon as how I do," Jared said, again touching her arm gently. "I'd like to go back someday too. Fact is, I didn't want to leave . . . but there was no choice. I understand, Kristy. Someday you'll get all you want out of life. And that's a promise."

Kristy got up and said, "We better go now, Papa, before Mamma has to come and fetch us. She'll be worried."

He pushed himself up slowly and then followed Kristy back into the hammock.

It was after ten o'clock when the yellow Mark IV turned off the highway and entered the hammock. Jared had been pacing back and forth beside the van for hours, desperately worried that perhaps the man at the service station had played a cruel joke on him, that no one would come looking for him. He almost ran to meet the automobile as it stopped beside a cabbage palm.

A huge man got out and leaned against the front of the car. He was almost six and a half feet tall, and weighed over two hundred and fifty pounds. His hair was red and short-cropped, and his face was almost as red as his hair. He looked to be around fifty years old. He studied Jared carefully and said, "You the folks who're looking for work?"

"Yes," Jared said nervously. "I'm Jared Teeter. Folks call me Jay."

The man snorted and said, "Your last name should have been Bird. Then folks could call you Jay Bird." He looked at Jared closely again and asked, "Where you folks from?"

"West Virginny. We just got down here a few days ago. I met the man at the service station yesterday when I tried to get a job there."

"You got any kin folk around here?"

"No. All our kin is back in West Virginny."

The man seemed to be in deep thought for a moment, and then he said, "I'm Silas Creedy. You ever picked before?"

Jared scratched his head, remembering that this same question had cost him a job once before. He finally said, "Yes, sir, I've done a good bit of it. I owned my own farm, and I've picked plenty of corn and vegetables."

"I mean picking. Worked the fields down here."

"Well, no, I guess not," Jared said uneasily, "but I can do anythin' I'm a mind to do. I'd sure like to try pickin' or anythin' else you want me to do."

Creedy looked toward the van. "Are them younguns healthy?" he asked.

"Yes. They's fine kids."

"But you got your old lady's belly swole up."

"She's 'bout seven months along."

"We don't usually allow nobody in the camp who can't work."

Jared had a sinking feeling that he was not going to get the job. He said quickly, "Her bein' that way won't bother my workin'. She's a good woman, and she can look after herself durin' the day."

Creedy remained silent for a moment, then he said, "Well, I guess you folks will do. Maybe your woman can find something to do around the camp during the day."

"The camp?" Jared asked quizzically.

"Yeah, the camp. You folks will live in my labor camp. It's called Angel City."

"You mean we get housin' too?" Jared asked, surprised.

"Yeah, you get housing," Creedy said impatiently. "How many times do I have to tell you, fellow? You'll live in my labor camp."

"Why, that's fine, Mr. Creedy," Jared said, "just fine. I was awful worried 'bout where we would find a place to stay." He hesitated for a moment, and then he asked, "Mr. Creedy, how much does this work pay?"

"Depends on you," Creedy answered. "Tomatoes pays twenty-five cents a bucket. Other stuff generally pays by the hamper. If we pick fruit, it's by the tub. The more you work the more you make. It's up to you."

"What about the cost of the camp housin'?"

"Ah, there's a little charge for that, but it don't amount

to much of nothing. We take it out of your earnings ev'ry Saturday when you get paid. You get supper cooked at the camp, but you have to look out for yourself for breakfast and whatever you eat in the fields at noon."

"That sounds fair enough," Jared said. "I'd be mighty proud to work fer you, Mr. Creedy."

Creedy then said, "Before we go to the camp I want you to follow me back to Florida City and get signed up for food stamps."

The statement puzzled Jared. He said, "Mr. Creedy, I don't need no food stamps. I've never taken charity in my lifetime. Mountain folk don't take charity."

"It's not charity!" Creedy snapped, annoyed by Jared's unexpected answer. "It's coming to you from your taxes. Ev'rybody at Angel City gets food stamps. All you have to do is sign up, and I take care of it from there. It won't be any bother to you."

"Well, I guess I'll do it if you say so. But we don't take charity from nobody."

"You just follow me back to Florida City, and then we'll go to the camp and get you folks set up."

The Dodge van followed the Mark IV as it left the highway and moved slowly along a dirt road surrounded on both sides by tomato fields. A small island of Australian pines broke the openness of the field about a mile south of the highway. When they reached the camp, Creedy got out, unlocked the gate and opened it. To the right of the gate there was a sign painted in red and blue that read:

ANGEL CITY
LABOR CAMP
POSITIVELY NO TRESPASSING
— *KEEP OUT* —

The camp covered about two acres of ground and was surrounded by an eight-foot chain link fence with three strands of barbed wire on top. The main building was a long concrete block structure with rows of doors on both the north and south sides, but no windows. Dingy whitewash hung in flaked strips from the concrete, and the roof overhang was sagging badly from rot. Behind this building there was a small block building containing a toilet and shower, and a house trailer was parked beneath the Australian pines in the south corner of the compound. A red pickup truck sat beside the trailer. The place seemed to be deserted except for an old Negro man sitting on the ground beneath one of the trees. He did not look up as the two vehicles entered and parked.

Creedy got out of the car and said, "You folks will have number ten on the north side. You can spend the rest of the afternoon getting settled. The bus will leave for the fields at six o'clock in the morning." With that he drove out, locked the gate and created a cloud of white limestone dust as he raced the Mark IV back toward the highway.

Bennie said, "How come he locked the gate, Papa? We can't get back outside if we want to."

Jared was also puzzled by this. He said, "I don't rightly know. Maybe they don't want folks in here that don't have no business bein' here when ev'rybody is in the fields. That might be a good idea."

They all followed Jared as he walked to the north side of the building and found a door with the number 10 painted above it. He opened the door and entered slowly. A naked light bulb with a string hanging down was in the center of the room. He pulled the string and flooded the eight-foot square cubicle with yellowish light. The heat and the strong smell of stale urine and vomit almost turned his stomach. He jumped back quickly and said, "Phew! We better let some air get in there afore we go in. That place smells like it's real ripe."

They waited for about five minutes and then entered again. The room was totally bare except for two sets of bunk beds against the walls. A pile of empty wine bottles was in one corner and was surrounded by dried vomit.

Jared held his nose and said, "We better get back out of here! I purely can't stand it!"

For several minutes they huddled silently outside the room, and then Jared said dejectedly, "It looks like I done got us in a real mess, don't it?"

"It wouldn't be so bad if it was just cleaned up," Cloma said, trying to ease the guilt in Jared's voice.

"It ain't goin' to be much even when it's cleaned up," he said.

"Why don't you ask that old man under the tree for some soap and a mop? And tomorrow we can get some spray that will take the bad smell out."

"I'll go and see to it now," Jared said.

The old Negro seemed to be asleep as Jared walked up to him. He appeared to be about eighty years old, and his body was nothing more than wrinkled skin and bones. Jared shook his arm and he looked up.

"Where can I get some soap and a mop?" Jared asked. "We want to clean the room."

The old man said, "I's de cook. I don' pick no 'maters no mo, an' I gits two bottles o' wine 'stead o' one. Dey's a mop in de outhouse but ev'rybody buys dey own soap."

Jared said, "You got some soap I can borrow 'til we can buy some? Or I could just buy it from you."

The old man answered, "I's de cook. I don' pick no 'maters no mo, an' I gits two bottles o' wine 'stead o' one. You'll have to go to de sto'."

"But the gate's locked and I can't get out," Jared said, becoming exasperated.

"I's de cook. I don' pick no 'maters no mo, an' . . . ."

Jared turned quickly and walked back to the room. He

said, "That old fool seems to be daffy. We'll just have to wait 'til somebody gets back to the camp. We might as well go sit under a tree where it's cooler."

They all walked to one of the Australian pines and sat on the soft needles that covered the ground. Jared said, "I been doin' some thinkin'. This place is worse than our old hawg pen, but we don't have to stay here long. If they pay twenty-five cents fer pickin' a bucket of tomatoes, and I can pick a hundred in a day, that's twenty-five dollars. If Kristy and Bennie can pick fifty each, that's another twenty-five bucks, or fifty dollars fer the day. For six days' work that's three hundred dollars — more clear money than I ever made in a month. At that rate it won't take us no time at all to have our own fruit stand. You think we can stick it out fer a few weeks?"

"I'll pick more than fifty, Papa," Bennie said with excitement.

"And I'll pick as many as Bennie," Kristy said.

"You won't neither," Bennie shot back. "You're just a girl. Can't no girl do nothin' like a man."

"We can make do all right, Jay," Cloma said assuredly. "The room won't be so bad once we get it cleaned up and the smell out."

Jared felt relief. He was afraid they would all hold it against him for bringing them to such a place. He said, "Well, it's settled then. We'll stick it out fer awhile, and we'll fill a bucket full of money afore you know it. We'll sell fruits and vegetables and pot-holders and aprons and Bennie can carve those little wooden animals he's so good at. It won't take us no time at all."

It was just before six when the two old school buses came into the camp and parked beside the trailer. One was painted a faded red and one blue. Both were covered with dust. On the side of one there was a sign painted in white: ANGEL CITY UNIT 1; on the other, ANGEL CITY UNIT 2.

About sixty people got out of the buses. All were black males except for ten black women, a white man and woman, and a white boy about the same age as Bennie. Some of the people ran and formed a line in front of the shower stall; others disappeared into their rooms; and some just plopped down to the ground and sat.

Jared and his family watched this sudden activity with curiosity, and then they walked back to the building and sat on the ground in front of their room. A black man was sitting in front of the door next to them.

In a few minutes a huge black man carrying a box walked down the side of the building. He handed each person a pint bottle of white wine. When he came to Jared he held the bottle in his outstretched hand and said nothing.

Jared looked up at him and said, "What's this?"

The man jabbed the bottle at Jared and remained silent.

The black man sitting on the ground by the adjacent room watched for a moment, and then he said, "Mistuh, you're payin' a buck-fifty for that bottle of junk whether you take it or not. You better take it."

"But I don't want any wine," Jared said, puzzled by the whole thing.

"You better take it. It'll help you get through the night."

Jared took the bottle, and then the huge black man continued on along the line of rooms. Jared turned the bottle over and over in his hands, staring at it, and then he said to the black man sitting next to him, "You want it?"

"You keep it. You'll need it sooner or later."

Jared took a closer look at this stranger. He was in his early forties, and the coal-black skin of his face was broken by a long white scar running down his left cheek. His clothes and shoes were covered with white dust.

No black people had ever lived anywhere near Teeter

Ridge, and Jared had never really known any. He was curious to know more about this black man, so he extended his hand and said, "My name's Jared Teeter. Folks call me Jay."

The black man was surprised by the extended hand. He reached over reluctantly, touched Jared for only a moment and then said, "I's called Cy."

For a moment neither of them said anything further, then the black man said, "Where you come from, Mistuh Jay?"

"West Virginny," Jared answered.

"What part of West Virginny?"

"Well, my place was out from Dink."

"Dink?" the man questioned. "What's that near?"

"Well, Dink's not far from Wallback or Valley Fork or Big Otter. Big Otter is close to Nebo, and Nebo is close to Mudfork, and Mudfork is close to . . . ."

"That be's all right," Cy interrupted. "You don't need to explain it no further."

Another period of silence prevailed, and then Jared said, "We can't go in the room, it stinks so bad. I got to have some soap and a mop. When do we go to the store?"

"We stops at the sto' comin' in ev'ry afternoon."

"Can't I go tonight after supper?"

The black man stared curiously at Jared, and then he said, "Only in the afternoon comin' in from the fields. But I got some soap powder you can have, an' they's a mop out by the shower stalls."

Just then an old black man with a white beard came out of Cy's room. He was singing an almost incoherent tune, "I seen Jesus today . . . I seen Jesus in de 'mater patch . . . I seen Jesus today . . . an' Jesus wuz pickin' 'maters . . . ."

Jared stared curiously at the old man as he walked away, still singing.

Cy turned to him and said, "Don't pay no never mind to him. He's tetched, but he don't bother nobody. Ev'rybody 'round here calls him Rude."

"Ain't he kind of old to be workin' in the fields?" Jared asked.

"That old man's past eighty, but he's like a machine. You point him down a tomato row an' he'll pick fo' buckets while anybody else picks one. He's been here three years now, an' if he wadden' so good at pickin', Creedy would-a kilt him a long time ago. I'll get yo soap."

Cy's last statement about the old man and Creedy baffled Jared and was totally beyond any degree of comprehension, but before Jared could question him further, Cy vanished into the room. He returned shortly and handed a box of soap powder to Jared.

"I sure thank you fer this," Jared said. "I'll pay you back tomorrow when I get to the store."

"Don't worry 'bout it. I don't use much soap no more."

"Well, I guess I'll go now and find the mop, and see what we can do with that room," Jared said.

"You best wait 'til after supper. It's 'bout that time, an' if'n you don't et when it's ready, you won't git none."

Cy leaned back against the wall and opened his bottle of wine. Jared watched as he put the bottle to his mouth and drained it in one gulp. He belched loudly, and then he looked at Jared and said, "That cheap junk cost forty-nine cents a pint at the sto', an' we pays Creedy a buck-fifty fo' it here in the camp ev'ry afternoon, whether we wants to buy it or not. Ain't that some crap?"

A loud clanging noise suddenly erupted from somewhere west of the barracks. Cy jumped up and said, "That's it. You gotta hav yo own plates an' foks." Then he hurried around the side of the barracks.

Jared went to the van and brought back a box containing plates and other utensils, and then they all joined a line leading to an open shed in the west corner of the camp. The stove was an iron grate propped up on concrete blocks. A wood fire smoldered beneath it, and three large blackened pots sat on top of the grate.

The frail old man who had called himself the cook was standing behind the grate, dipping from the pots as each person came past. Onto each plate he dumped a glob of boiled pork backbone, a portion of boiled squash and stewed tomatoes, and two slices of white bread. The old man had no teeth, and his mouth popped constantly as he served the food.

Some of the people took their plates back to their rooms, and others squatted on the ground close by the shed. Jared and his family went to a tree by the side of the van. The sun had now sunk deeply into the western horizon, and two floodlights came on at each end of the building.

For a moment they ate in silence, and then Jared said solemnly, "If that old man's a cook, then I'm one of them ballet dancers."

Cloma smiled as Bennie said, "This squash tastes like it's got sand in it."

"He didn't wash it before he cooked it," Cloma said. "Maybe now you'll appreciate more the good food I've been givin' you all this time."

Jared laughed and said, "Well, ev'rybody save a little bit fer Skip. Maybe he can eat it."

Kristy said, "Papa, Skip can have all of mine if he wants it. I'm just not hungry."

When they finished what they could eat of the supper, they joined another line leading to the hydrant close by the side of the outhouse where people were washing their dishes. Jared got a bucket from the van, filled it with water, looked for the mop and found it in the shower stall. Then he went back to the room.

He put the mop and bucket against the wall, and then he said to Cloma, "You want me to help with this?"

"No," she answered. "Bennie and Kristy can do it. I'll watch and see that it's done right."

"You ought not do any work yourself. I'll help if you say so." He moved toward her.

"You'd just be in the way. We can't hardly turn around in this little room as it is. We'll do it."

Jared then left the room and walked to the fence on the north side of the camp. Far in the distance he could see the glow of lights hovering above Florida City and Homestead, creating a huge yellow dome in the darkness of the sky. His thoughts began to drift back again to the farm in West Virginia.

He was startled when he realized that Cy was standing beside him. His body jerked as he spun around.

"I didn't mean to scare you," Cy said.

"That's o.k. I was just thinkin', and I didn't hear you come up."

Cy leaned against the fence, and then he said slowly, "Mistuh, I don't knows how you come to be in here, but you seems like a good man. You ought to take yo woman an' them younguns an' git outen here the fust thing in the mornin' while you still can."

"I don't understand what you're sayin'," Jared said, puzzled.

"I mean, git outen here! You ain't got no business in Angel City!"

"I can't do that," Jared said, even more puzzled by the insistence of this black man he didn't even really know. Then he said emphatically, "I need the work!"

Cy suddenly turned and carefully searched the area next to the barracks. He noticed that the huge black man who had passed out the bottles of wine was standing near the flood-light on the east end of the building. He turned back again and faced Jared as if he had something more to say; but then he wheeled around quickly and walked back toward his room.

FIVE

DAWN HAD not come the next morning when Angel City came to life. Little fires sprang up in front of doors, and people moved about beneath the dim glow of the floodlights like vague shadows. The smell of coffee drifted through the camp.

Jared stepped from the room and breathed deeply of the cool air, trying to shake the sleep from his head. He had spent a restless night in the concrete cubicle which still reeked with a foul odor. Cy was sitting on the ground beside a fire. He had propped a grille on top of four blackened beer cans, and a small coffee pot bubbled over the flames. The old man called Rude was eating sardines from a can.

Jared looked at Cy and said, "Good mornin'."

"Mornin'," Cy replied.

"Where'd you get the wood fer the fire?" Jared asked.

"Out by the cookshed. They's a pile of branches out there."

Jared went to the shed and returned with a bundle of sticks. By the time the fire came to life, Cloma came outside.

She looked at the fire and said, "How'm I goin' to make coffee over that? We don't have a grille to set the pot on."

"Just set the pot in the fire," Jared said. "I'll take the grille off the camp stove in the van when we get back this afternoon."

Cy looked up and said, "You can use my grille now. I'm through with it. And they's water in the bucket by the wall."

Cloma boiled coffee over the glowing coals, and when Kristy and Bennie came from the room, they all sat on the ground and ate the sweet buns left from the day before. Cy opened a can of Vienna sausage.

Jared looked at Cloma and said, "Do we have any food left to take to the field?"

"Nothin' but a few oranges," she replied.

"I can let you have three cans of sardines," Cy said. "That's all I can spare. But you can eat all the tomatoes you wants in the field."

"I'd appreciate the sardines," Jared said. "I could have brought more food if I had known. We'll leave a can of sardines fer Cloma, and maybe the cook will have something else she can have."

"He won't have nothin' fo' nobody 'til supper," Cy said.

"Don't worry about me," Cloma said. "I'll do fine with sardines and oranges. It's you I'm worried about. You can't work all day without proper food."

"I've always liked tomatoes," Jared said. "I'll probably eat a bushel."

"You'll sho' be stopped up if'n you do," Cy said. He then looked at Jared and said seriously, "You folks better go out back an' relieve yo'selves afore we go to the fields. They ain't no place in the fields to do a job excepin' in front of ev'rybody."

Jared gave the black man a queer look. He said, "Well, thanks fer the information. That's good to know."

Bennie then jumped up and ran toward the outhouse.

Promptly at six a clanging sound came from the area of the cook shed, and people moved immediately toward the two buses. Those who lived in the north side of the barracks were assigned to Unit 1, and those on the south side to Unit 2. A driver stood by each bus, counting the people as they entered. Jared, Kristy and Bennie climbed aboard Unit 1.

Dawn was just breaking when the buses turned onto the highway and headed east. They drove for three miles and then turned north on a narrow paved farm road. Fields seemingly stretched into infinity on both sides of the road, fields that had once been part of the impenetrable Everglades but had been wrenched violently from nature, diked, drained, and stripped bare of flora and fauna, marshland turned into arid soil that now formed one of America's largest vegetable gardens. Each day an army of men and women swarmed across the land, a conglomerate of lifetime migrants and exiles from failure and defeat in rural areas of Appalachia and the Carolinas and Georgia and Tennessee and Alabama. From the green vines they plucked hundreds of thousands of tomatoes that were processed in Florida City and Homestead and then shipped to distant markets to be served in salads and sandwiches in New York and Boston and Chicago and Minneapolis and Detroit and New Orleans and Denver and Toronto.

They also passed fields planted heavily with pole beans and squash and okra and potatoes and cucumbers and peppers. All of the fields were dotted with white splotches as egrets searched for their breakfast.

In some of the tomato fields, the rows were covered with strips of white plastic to hold in moisture and to kill weeds, and the plants grew from holes in the strips. From a distance, these fields looked as if they were covered with snow.

The buses finally turned into the edge of a field and parked beside a row of Australian pines. A flatbed truck loaded with empty crates was parked nearby. As each person was issued a bucket, they selected a row and moved out into the field like lines of advancing soldiers. The flatbed truck followed slowly behind the mass of pickers.

For the first two hours, the picking was like an adventuresome game to Kristy and Bennie. They felt tinges of excitement each time they plucked a tomato from a plant and gradually filled a bucket. They almost ran as they took the buckets back to the truck and dumped them into a crate. But as the sun moved higher into the sky, intensifying the heat reflecting from the rocky soil, they began to move slower and slower and fill the buckets less often.

About mid-morning, Cy came up alongside Kristy and said to her, "Little miss, I been watchin' you. You better take it easy, else you gone be laid out afore noon. It's a long day in the fields when you not use to it. You stay alongside o' me fo' a while an' I'll pick some in yo' bucket."

"That wouldn't be fair," Kristy said, wiping sweat from her forehead with the back of her hand. "That would be taking away from you."

"That don't matter none at all," he said. "You just stay alongside me fo' awhile."

For a half-hour she stayed abreast of the black man as he picked into two buckets at once, and then she began to fall behind. She finally sat down to rest as the other pickers moved farther and farther away from her.

At noon the workers took a half-hour break. Jared, Kristy and Bennie sat on the ground and shared the two cans of sardines. They also ate two tomatoes each. Water was available from a keg on the back of the truck.

By mid-afternoon, even Jared was hurting. The rows became longer and longer, and the buckets bigger and bigger. His shirt was drenched with sweat as he too fell farther and farther behind the experienced pickers.

It was a long walk back to the buses when the day finally ended at five. The smell of sweat-soaked bodies was almost overpowering as the bus lumbered back along the narrow farm road. A mile east of the camp the buses pulled into a parking area adjacent to a concrete block building housing the Gater General Store.

As each person got off the bus, the driver handed them a dollar bill. Cy explained to Jared that this was an advance on earnings to buy food for the next day. The pickers pushed into the store and made purchases quickly. Some returned to the buses drinking cans of cold beer, while others carried brown paper bags containing sardines or Vienna sausage or pickled pigs' feet or slices of hoop cheese or cans of beans or loaves of white bread.

Cloma ran to meet them when Jared, Kristy and Bennie got off the bus inside the camp. They walked back to the room slowly. Kristy and Bennie grabbed towels and went immediately to join the line leading to the shower stall.

Jared sat on one of the bunks and groaned. "I never knowed that pickin' tomatoes could be so rough," he said wearily to Cloma. "My back feels like it's broke. And I know it was tough on them two younguns, but they really tried hard."

"Did you do as well as you hoped you would?" Cloma asked.

"Nope. But we'll do better as we get used to it. I picked eighty-two buckets, Bennie got forty, and Kristy got twenty-seven. That's not too bad, though. One more bucket and we'd have made forty dollars today."

"I hope it won't be long," Cloma said. "Me and that old cook were the only people here today. I tried to talk to him once, but all he would say was some gibberish about him bein' the cook and not havin' to pick anymore. Skip was a real comfort to me. I even got to talkin' to him."

The small dog was lying on a blanket Cloma had placed for him under a bunk.

The giant black man suddenly came into the room and

handed Jared a pint of white wine. Jared took it without comment and sat it against the wall beside the other bottle.

Cloma said, "That's another bad thing here. You just can't have any privacy at all. If you shut the door it's like an oven, and if you leave it open people just walk by and look right in. Did you get the spray?"

"Yes." Jared reached into a brown paper bag and handed her a can of aerosol spray. "But I didn't buy any food except in cans. We can't keep meat or anything like that without a refrigerator or ice. We'll just have to make do fer awhile as best we can."

Cloma started spraying the deodorant around the room. She said, "I scrubbed this place three more times today just to have somethin' to do. It's plenty clean now. But we've got to have some chairs. I can't even sit outside durin' the day 'less I sit on the ground."

"Maybe we can go into town Saturday afternoon and look in the used furniture stores," Jared said. He knew that staying alone all day in the small room was a cruel hardship for her.

"That would be nice. A used chair ought not cost too much."

Jared took a towel from a cardboard box. "I've got to get this white dust off'n me," he said. "It itches worse than pison ivy. I've never seen fields so full of rocks and dust. I don't see how they make things grow at all, but they do. The rocks are nearbouts as thick as a mountain crick bed. We'll have to get better shoes. But I noticed that some of the black people were barefooted. They must have feet like iron."

"They're probably used to it," Cloma said. "And besides that, I've always heard that black folks are as tough as nails."

"They must be. It hurt me clear through the soles of my shoes. But you know, I seen a strange thing today. I looked up two or three times and the black man in the room next to us — the one called Cy — he was pickin' into Kristy's bucket."

"How come him to do that?"

"I don't know, 'less he figured she needed some help and he was willin' to give it. But it looks to me like that would cost him money." Jared got up, stretched, and said, "I'm goin' now and take a bath afore the supper bell rings." He looked back. "That stuff sure makes the room smell better."

The meal that night consisted of fried strips of salt pork, pole beans and stewed tomatoes. All of the Teeters ate on the ground outside their room. When they were finished, Kristy and Bennie walked away to explore the camp, and Cloma went to the hydrant beside the outhouse to wash the day's dirty underclothes. Jared leaned back against the wall as Skip came from the room and sat beside him. He reached over and patted the dog's head.

Cy was also sitting on the ground in front of his room. He looked at Jared and said, "What you call that mutt?"

"His name's Skip," Jared answered. "He's 'bout the best rabbit dog you've ever seen. If they's a rabbit within ten miles, he'll find him."

"They don't 'low no dogs in here," Cy said. "You best get rid of him."

"I couldn't do that. We've had him over eight years."

"You could take him outside when the gate opens in the mornin' an' turn him loose."

"He wouldn't go nowhere," Jared said. "He'd just hang around out there and starve."

"You could take him to the fields an' turn him loose. He'd find a home sommers."

Jared was becoming agitated by the conversation. He snapped, "This little dog won't bother nobody! We'll keep him in the room as much as possible, and he won't hurt a soul!"

"It's yo' dog," Cy said with finality.

Both men remained silent for several minutes, then Jared looked back to Cy and said quizzically, "What does Mr.

Creedy get out of all this?"

Cy gave Jared a piercing look. For a moment he didn't answer, and then he muttered, "Plenty."

"In what way?" Jared asked, wanting to know more about the operation of the camp.

Cy glanced down the side of the building, and then he leaned closer and said, "He's a contractor. He gits two dollars an' fifty cents an hour fo' hisself fo' all the time we're in the fields ev'ry day. And he also gits a dollar each fo' ev'ry picker he puts in the fields ev'ry day. That's a heap o' money, but it ain't enough fo' Creedy. If'n he could figger a way to haul out ev'rybody's do-do from the shithouse an' sell it fo' fertilizer, he'd do it!"

Jared figured briefly in his mind and said, "That is a lot of money fer Creedy, but he's got the expense of this camp and the food at night and the buses."

Cy gave Jared another piercing look. He grunted but did not comment further about Creedy.

Jared then asked, "Who're those two men who drive the buses and hand out the wine?"

Cy said, "The big 'un is called Jabbo, an' the one with the twisted nose is Clug."

"How come they don't pick?" Jared asked.

"Them's Creedy's men. They live in the trailer. They ain't pickers. An' you best stay clear of them two. They's mean niggers." Cy then got up and said, "I'm goin' walk aroun' some. I'll see you later." He was tired of Jared's questions.

Jared got up and put Skip in the room, then he walked around the end of the building. He had wanted to meet the white family living in the south side of the barracks.

He found them sitting on the ground in front of a room. The man was about four years younger than Jared, the woman the same age as Cloma, and the boy was Bennie's age. The man had a sullen look on his face.

Jared squatted in front of them and said, "Howdy. My

name's Jared Teeter. Folks call me Jay." He extended his hand.

The man ignored Jared's offered handshake and said in a flat tone, "What you want?"

Jared was surprised by the reaction. He said, "I don't want nothin'. I just thought I'd visit a spell. We just got here yesterday. We come from West Virginny."

The man became even more sullen. He said, "You come around here 'cause we're white too?"

"No," Jared answered, feeling uncomfortable and wishing he had not even tried to start a conversation with the stranger. "That had nothin' to do with it. I just wanted to visit."

"If you think you're goin' to get special treatment in here 'cause you're white, you can forget it." The man's tone was now hostile. "Creedy don't give a damn if you're white or black or purple. You're just two more hands in the field, that's all. Just two more hands in the field. You won't get nothin' special in here 'cause you're white."

Jared was startled by the outburst, and then it angered him. He said firmly, "I ain't lookin' fer no special favors! I've always pulled my own weight! We's mountain folk!"

"You damned well better pull your own weight!" the man snapped harshly.

Jared had had enough. As he jumped up to leave, the boy looked at him and said, "My pa here is Willard Baxley. My ma is Martha. I'm Lonnie. We come from Alabama." His tone was apologetic.

"I hear that's a good place," Jared said, not knowing what else to say. "It's good to have met you folks." He then turned and walked away quickly.

Cloma had returned to the room when Jared came inside, but Bennie and Kristy were not there. Cloma said, "There's no place for me to hang these wet clothes. The fence is too high, and there's not a single clothes line in the camp."

"Just drape 'em over the side of the bunks," Jared said.

"The heat in here will dry 'em in no time." He was still feeling puzzled and dejected by the man's reaction to his offered friendship.

Cloma said, "We've just got to get an electric fan, Jay. My bunk was soaked with sweat when I got up this morning."

Jared acted as if he did not hear her. Skip came from under the bunk, and he reached down and patted the dog's head. For a moment he pulled at the dog's ears, and then he said, "It's best you look after Skip real good. They's things here I don't understand. You best keep him close to you durin' the day."

"How come he needs special treatment all of a sudden?" Cloma asked. "He can't go anywhere with that fence out there and the gate locked."

"It's just best that you watch after him real good," Jared insisted.

Kristy and Bennie then came running into the room. Bennie's face was flushed with excitement as he said, "We been out to the south side of the camp, Papa, behind the cook shed. Mister Cy was there. He said that the marsh you can see beyond the south field is the Everglades. He said there's alligators out there. Will you take us to see an alligator, Papa? We ain't never seen one."

Jared looked at Bennie's flushed face. He said, "Maybe we can take a hike out there Sunday afternoon. But I don't know if the alligators are there or not."

"Mister Cy said they were," Bennie exclaimed.

Kristy said, "Mister Cy picked in my bucket. He helped me, Papa. I don't think he would tell us about the alligators if it wasn't true."

Jared was pleased that his children were in a happy mood. He said, "Well, if Mister Cy said it, I guess it must be so. We'll go out there Sunday afternoon, and we'll see the alligators then."

"Maybe we can catch a little one and keep him for a pet,"

Bennie said. "Nobody back in Dink ever had a pet alligator."

Jared then got up from the bunk and left the room. He suddenly felt a need to be alone for a few minutes. Night had now come, and he walked out to the north fence and watched the glow of lights in the eastern sky. Occasionally, a car passed along the highway a mile from the camp, its headlights slicing the darkness. Muted sounds drifted outward from the barracks.

When he turned to leave, Jared noticed that Jabbo was standing in the edge of the darkness by the gate, watching him.

SIX

NEITHER JARED, Kristy nor Bennie did much better the remainder of the week than they had done the first day, but they were becoming more accustomed to the work. Jared knew he would improve as time went on, and that he would eventually pick as many tomatoes as anyone in the field. He had doubts only about Kristy, and he wished she did not have to go into the fields at all. He felt pity for the black women who worked each day, although he knew they had probably done this all of their lives.

By the end of Saturday, Jared figured their four-day total at six hundred and two buckets. This was not as high as he had hoped, but he knew it was not bad for their first effort. He believed they could reach a goal of two hundred buckets per day.

The bus went straight back to the camp and did not stop at the store. A half-hour after they had arrived, Creedy drove into the camp in the Mark IV. He had a gray metal cash box with him, and he sat in a chair behind a small table as a line formed.

When Jared finally reached the table, Creedy examined a ledger and then said to him, "Way I got it figured, your total is three hundred, seventy-two dollars and fifty cents."

Jared was surprised. He said, "Mr. Creedy, we didn't earn that much, did we? Not unless the pay was more than the twenty-five cents a bucket as you said it would be."

"I didn't say how much you *earned*," Creedy said. "The amount is what you *owe* me."

Jared was dumbfounded by the words. For a moment he couldn't speak. He finally said, "What did you say, Mr. Creedy?"

"You heard me!" Creedy snapped impatiently. "You owe me three hundred and seventy-two dollars and fifty cents."

Jared said, "There ain't no way I could do that! No way!"

Creedy glanced at the ledger and said, "Well, let's see. There's a fee of one hundred dollars for being put to work, and ev'rybody that stays in the camp pays this whether they works or not. That's four hundred dollars for you and your bunch. That's only a one-time charge. You don't have to pay it no more. Then there's ten dollars each per week for rent. That's forty bucks. And five dollars a week for electricity. The supper is two dollars each, so that's thirty-six bucks for the four days this week. The bus is two dollars a day each to the fields, and I give each one of you a one-dollar advance ev'ry day for food. The wine is a buck-fifty a bottle. That all figures out to five hundred and twenty-three dollars. You earned a hundred and fifty dollars and fifty cents picking, so you're into me for three hundred and seventy-two dollars and fifty cents. You understand now?"

Jared did not understand. His mind was completely addled by Creedy's rapid flow of figures, and to him the whole situation seemed to be unreal. He said, "How come you didn't tell me 'bout all them charges before we came in here? How come you didn't tell me?"

"Well, I'm sure I did. You just don't remember, or else

you wasn't paying attention like you should." Creedy then pushed the ledger aside and looked directly at Jared. "You want to settle this up now with cash, or do you want to work it out?" he asked, knowing that Jared probably did not have the money.

"I don't have that much," Jared replied, still unable to believe that what was happening was real. "We had some bad luck with the van comin' down here."

"Well," Creedy said condescendingly as he reached for the cash box, "it won't take you no time at all to clear the debt and then start making some real money. You'll see. So don't worry about it. I'm going to advance five dollars for you and two-fifty each for your younguns. Here's ten bucks." He handed Jared a ten-dollar bill.

Jared took the money and stepped out of the line. He turned it over and over in his hands, staring at it. Then he watched as each person came up to the table. Everyone was handed only a five-dollar bill for the week's work.

Cloma knew immediately that something was wrong when Jared came into the room. His face was drawn and white. He sat on the bunk and slumped forward, not speaking. She asked anxiously, "Jared? What is it, Jared?"

He tried to explain, but she did not understand the various figures Creedy had quoted any better than Jared did. She said worriedly, "What will we do, Jared?" She always called him Jared when they were discussing something serious or when something frightened her.

He said, "I don't know. I've only got around a hundred and fifty dollars left from the trip. We can't pay off the debt except by workin' it out. We'll just have to pick harder, I guess. I'm sorry I got all of you into such a mess as this."

Jared blinked as Jabbo stepped into the room and handed him the bottle of wine. He put it against the wall with the other bottles. There was no time for him to take a shower before the supper bell rang.

Soon after supper, everyone went to the buses for the usual Saturday trip to the store. Jared walked up to the giant black man and said, "We'll go in the van. I need to run it some to keep the battery up."

"You go in the bus," Jabbo said. "Ev'rybody goes in the bus."

Some of the people seemed almost happy as they reached the store with their five dollars in cash. Others were as grim as Jared. Some made food purchases, while others spent the money for a quart-bottle of whiskey.

Cloma found a small electric fan priced at eight dollars. She said to Jared, "Can we afford to buy this?"

"Yes. But I don't see any chairs at all."

"It doesn't matter," Cloma said. "There's some empty bean hampers behind the cook shed. I'll make myself a chair."

Jared purchased more canned food and a carton of eggs. Kristy and Bennie each spent twenty-five cents for candy, and then they went back to the bus.

Creedy drove up and parked in front of the store, and Jared went over to him. He said, "Mr. Creedy, are we allowed to go outside the camp on Sunday?"

"What for?" Creedy asked.

"Me and my folks are used to services on Sunday. I was a deacon back home."

Creedy chuckled and said, "Well, maybe you can get Jabbo or Clug to say a few words, and get that ding-bat cook to play the fiddle. Some of them niggers can probably sing, too."

"Are you sayin' we can't go?" Jared asked, not amused by Creedy's remarks.

"I got business to take care of," Creedy said impatiently. He turned and walked away briskly.

It was almost dark when the buses pulled back into the camp. Some of the people were already drunk as they headed for their rooms. Shrill laughter broke the usual silence of the compound, and the sound of scuffling came from some of the rooms.

Jared put his packages in the room, came back outside and sat on the ground. Cy was leaning back against the wall, drinking from a bottle of whiskey. He turned to Jared and said, "You want some?"

"No," Jared said. "But thanks anyway." He did not want to let his depression make him speak rudely.

Cy took another drink and said, "I worked a week in them fields fo' this bottle of whuskey, an' they won't be nothin' left of it by tomorrow but dried piss in the dust. A whole week's work shot right through my pecker an' down in the dust."

Jared picked up a stick and scratched absently at the ground. Cy watched for a moment, then he said, "Creedy's a fine man, ain't he? I tried to tell you."

"It won't take long," Jared said. "We'll work it out and be gone from here in no time."

Cy said, "I been here two years an' I ain't worked it out yet. I never seen nobody leave Angel City that didn't leave feet first. Excepin' for two Cubans. That's the only thing Creedy won't bring in here no mo'. Cubans."

"How's that?" Jared asked, mildly interested.

"He brought two of them Cubans in here 'bout six months ago, an' he worked 'em fo' a week an' wouldn't pay 'em. They couldn't hardly speak no English at all, but they was shoutin' all kinds of stuff at Creedy. Then they pulled out them long pig-stickers that Cubans carry. One of 'em held Jabbo an' Clug 'gainst the fence, an' the other one commences to carve his name on ole Creedy's fat belly. Then they took a whole sack o' money from that big Mark IV an' hightailed it out o' here. Creedy couldn't say nothin' 'bout it to the police, an' he knew that if he went over to Miami lookin' fo' them two Cubans, they'd be a hundred more jus' like 'em out lookin' fo' him with them long pig-stickers. So he jus' lets it be, an' then he comes back in here an' beats the hell outen six of us niggers."

"Where do all these people in here come from?" Jared asked.

"Ev'rywhere," Cy said, drinking again. "Creedy even goes up to the Carolinas an' brings folks down here. Promises 'em good jobs. One time I seen him bring a drunk nigger in here who was wearin' one of them red monkey suits like men wear in front of a hotel to open doors an' unload baggage. When he sobered up, he started raisin' hell. They beat that nigger like I ain't never seen befo', but he wouldn't shet up. They finally took him fo' a ride in the pickup."

"How did you get in here?" Jared asked, absorbed by Cy's tales.

The more Cy drank, the freer he seemed willing to talk. He said, "He got me in Belle Glade. He come by this camp where I was livin' an' got me drunk. The next thing I knowed, I was here in Angel City."

Jared said, "Well, if you've been here two years now, you couldn't possibly be still in debt to Creedy."

"You be's in debt if'n you stays here ten," Cy said.

Jared thought that most of the things Cy was saying was just whiskey talk. He said skeptically, "I don't believe that nobody has to stay here if they don't want to, no matter how much Creedy says they owe. If nothin' else, they could just break and run in the field."

"That's been tried befo', an' they always come after you. You ever been pistol-whupped?"

"No."

"It ain't a pretty sight, but it's even worse if'n you on the receivin' end of it."

Jared became silent for a moment, trying to digest all the things Cy was saying. Although he had never really known a black person, Jared had always heard that they always either exaggerate all that they say or outright lie. He could not determine if he should believe this black man or not, but he was interested in the things he was saying. He then said to Cy, "Are all the camps like this one?"

"No, they ain't all like Angel City." He took another drink, then he continued, "They's a few more like this where you can't get out if'n you want to, but it don't make no matter. You can't really get out of none of 'em, an' the livin' is just as bad if they's a gate or not. They all 'bout the same, an' I seen 'em all. I been a picker all my life, movin' from one place to another. I don't even know where I was born. It could 'a been in a tomato patch."

"If you're not bein' paid fer your work here after you've cleared your debt, I still don't see why you don't leave," Jared said stubbornly.

Cy took another deep drink from the bottle. He wiped his mouth and said, "I tried to get away two or three times. They whupped me good, but that just made me madder. But the last time I tried it, Creedy took my boy."

"What?" Jared asked, completely puzzled by this statement. "He did what?"

"He took my boy to stay at his place. He brings him out here ev'ry Sunday afternoon fo' a visit. He's got them white folks' little girl, too, an' five or six more younguns. You ain't goin' to run off with *that* over yo' head."

Jared couldn't bring himself to believe Cy's words. He said, "Nobody can do something like that to someone else. You could tell the police."

"I tell the police, they'll take my boy out in the swamp, in that pickup truck. They'll kill him an' dump him in a sink-hole, an' that'll be the end o' that. Me an' my woman, we made that baby right in the middle of a bean field at noon one day, an' later, when he was born, he was born right in the middle of a bean field. There wasn't no papers or records or nothin', so there ain't no way I could prove that I ever even had a boy."

Jared was again shocked by the words, but he still could not face the reality of what this black man was saying. He then said to Cy, "Where's your wife now? Is she with the boy?"

"She died eight years ago, when the boy was born. We was in the Carolinas, pickin' beans. Migrant folk can't afford one of them sto'-bought funerals, so I buried her out in the woods."

Suddenly Jared did believe. He knew that the black man was incapable of fabricating such a story. For a moment he gazed beyond the fence and across the darkness of the fields; then he turned to Cy and said, "Is this the way it's always been for people like you?"

"You mean nigger field hands?" Cy asked.

"Yes. I guess that's what I mean."

"It's always been the same, an' it goin' always be the same."

Jared said, "I'm sorry, Cy . . . I never knowed. I thought I'd seen all the hard times they was back on that ridge in West Virginny, but I guess I was just a dumb hillbilly. I never knowed what it was really like out here. I'm sorry." Then he got up and walked away quickly into the darkness.

SEVEN

JARED DID not tell Cloma about the conversation with Cy and the things he had said. He did not want her to know the real truth about Angel City or Creedy or for her to be aware of the seriousness of their situation. He was determined that he would pick more tomatoes than anyone in the camp, and work off the debt quickly. Then they would simply leave all this behind them.

Sunday was a long day. The buses did not make a trip to the store, and the gate remained locked. The monotony of the long hours of confinement within the camp became stifling.

Cloma made a Sunday morning breakfast of fried eggs. Jared asked Cy to join them, and he did so eagerly, saying that he had not eaten eggs in more than a year. They offered some to the old man, Rude, but he refused. He ate his usual breakfast of one can of sardines.

It was just after noon when Creedy brought the children to the camp. Jared watched with deep pity as the boy ran to Cy and grabbed him around the neck. Cy took the boy's hand, and they disappeared into their room. Jared now understood why the white man on the other side of the barracks had been so sullen and belligerent when he had visited him. It had not been hostility, but fear. He felt sorrow for all the families whose children had been taken from them, and he wondered what he would do if Creedy or anyone ever tried to take Kristy or Bennie.

Jared entered the field on Monday morning deeply troubled. He picked the tomatoes frantically, filling bucket after bucket, running to the truck and back again. Bennie and Kristy watched him with wonder. He did not even stop at noon when the two of them ate cans of Vienna sausage.

By quitting time he had picked a hundred and thirty-two buckets. Every bone and muscle in his body ached as he walked back to the bus. He also felt a gnawing hunger from not eating since before daylight that morning.

Kristy took a seat beside him. She looked at him distastefully and said, "Papa, you stink. How come you worked so fast today?"

He glanced at himself and noticed for the first time that his clothes were as wet as if he had fallen into a creek. He was also covered with white dust. Her innocent statement made him smile, and he said, "You know, Kristy, you're right. I do stink. I sure better have a bath afore your mother gets a whiff of me."

When they reached the store he purchased food for the next day, and he also bought a can of corned beef, which he wolfed down quickly during the trip from the store to the camp. As soon as he put the package in the room, he headed for the shower stall.

The meal that evening made Jared feel guilty for eating the corned beef and not sharing it. They were served boiled pork neck bones, squash and stewed tomatoes. All of them felt a certain amount of constant hunger, but Jared did not want to spend more than the three dollars a day they were advanced for food unless it became absolutely necessary. He wanted to keep the hundred and fifty dollars intact in case he needed it to help buy their way out of Angel City.

They took the plates back to the barracks and sat on the ground in front of their room. Skip came outside when he smelled the pork. Jared gave him a pile of bones, and he chewed them ravenously. Jared watched for a moment, and then he said to no one in particular, "At least he don't have to eat no stewed tomatoes. I'm gettin' pretty damned sick of 'em, and ripe ones too fer that matter."

Cy was sitting close by, his plate untouched as he finished the bottle of wine. He said to Jared, "This slop they feed us ain't nothin' but the trash they throw out from the packin' plants in Homestead. Creedy gets it in a big garbage can ev'ry day. An' the stuff he does buy, like the salt bacon an' neck bones, he buys it with them food stamps he makes ev'rybody sign up for. It don't cost him nothin'!"

"I used to feed my hawgs better," Jared said, "but I guess folks sommers would be glad to even get this. But it sure do cut down a man's pleasure at meal-time."

Kristy put her plate aside and said, "Papa, if I wrote my name on some of the tomatoes I pick, do you reckon anybody would ever know that I picked them?"

"I guess they might," Jared answered. "But it would be mighty hard to write on a tomato. And they wouldn't have no way of knowing where you are nohow. Folks don't think about where somethin' comes from when they eat it. They jus' eat it, that's all."

"Well, they ought to," Kristy said. "Pickin' is hard work. I might try putting my name on the tomatoes."

Cloma said, "Is Mr. Creedy still here?"

"He was out by the trailer a few minutes ago," Jared said, curious as to why she had asked. "What you want with him?"

"I wrote a letter today to Mamma and Papa. Maybe he'll mail it for me."

Jared got up and said, "I'll go and see."

Kristy said, "I got a letter too, Papa, to Jeff. Will you ask him to mail it too?"

Jared smiled and said, "I thought somethin' pretty serious was goin' on between you and Jeff. So that's why you want to go back to the mountains. Let me have the letter and I'll send it along too."

Kristy blushed as she went into the room and came back with the letter.

When Jared came around the side of the building, the Mark IV was still there. He knocked on the door of the trailer and Creedy came outside. Jared said, "Can you mail a couple of letters fer me, Mr. Creedy?"

"Yeah," Creedy replied.

"I don't have no stamps, but here's two dimes."

"I'll mail 'em when I get back to Homestead," Creedy said. He stepped back into the trailer.

As soon as Jared was gone, Creedy ripped the letters in half and threw them into a waste basket.

It was the next morning when he went out to the cook shed to get firewood that Jared found Skip. The little dog's head had been severed, and was lying about four feet from the body. Jared had not seen Skip in the darkness but had stumbled over the body. He lit a match and discovered that he was standing in a pool of dried blood. For a moment he did not move, then he stooped down and touched the bloody form.

Jared picked up the body and the head and placed them on the ground beside the van. Then he went to the trailer and knocked on the door. Jabbo looked out and said, "Whut you want?"

"Who killed my dog?" Jared demanded angrily.

"Whut dawg?"

"You know damned well what dog!"

"I don't know nothin' 'bout no dawg."

Jabbo started to close the door, but Jared pushed it back violently and demanded, "Who killed him, dammit, you or Clug?"

The giant black man glared at Jared menacingly. He said harshly, "White man, you better move on away from here!"

Jared let his better judgment overcome his anger. He stepped back and said, "I'll need a shovel to bury him."

"You ain't buryin' no dawg inside this camp," Jabbo said. "Mistuh Creedy don't 'low that. You can take him outside the fence an' bury him when we gits back this afternoon."

"I'm not leavin' Skip on the ground all day!" Jared said defiantly. "I'll not leave this camp 'til he's buried!"

Jabbo glared at Jared again and said threateningly, "White man, if'n you ain't on that bus when we leave this mo'nin', I'll bust yo' ass wide open!" Then he slammed the door.

Jared stood there for a moment, and then he went back to the room. Cloma was standing in the doorway, holding the coffee pot. She said anxiously, "Where's the sticks for the fire, Jay? I been waitin' on you. You won't have much time now to eat breakfast."

He ignored her remarks and said, "Skip's dead. Somebody killed him out by the cook shed."

"What?" she said with disbelief. "Why would anybody do that to Skip?"

Bennie and Kristy had heard what Jared had said. "Where is he now, Papa?" Bennie asked. "I want to see."

"He's out by the van, but don't go there. His head's been cut off, and it ain't a pretty sight."

Kristy fell across the bunk and started crying as Bennie ran from the room. Jared shouted, "I said no, Bennie! Don't go out there!"

Bennie stopped and looked back. "I want to see," he repeated.

"No!" Jared said again. "I'll have to wait 'til this afternoon to bury him."

Bennie came back to the room reluctantly. "Who done it, Papa?" he asked, anger in his voice.

"I don't know. It was probably Jabbo or Clug. Cy told me that Creedy don't allow dogs in the camp, but I didn't listen. I guess it's my fault he's dead, but I didn't think nobody would do a thing like this."

"They didn't have to kill him," Bennie said, now trying hard to hold back the tears.

Jared went into the room and put his arm around Kristy. She sat up and leaned against him, and then she said, "I'm sorry, Papa. I didn't mean to cry."

"Ev'rybody cries," Jared said. "Even a man cries sometimes." He brushed his hand against her cheek.

Cloma said, "You all better eat somethin' now. There's no time left for makin' coffee."

Kristy and Bennie both ate a cinnamon bun, but Jared took nothing. He went back to the van and covered Skip's body with brown paper. When he returned to the room Bennie said, "Will we say words over him, Papa?"

"Yes. We'll say words."

Cy had watched it all but said nothing.

When they reached the field, Jared again picked frantically. By mid-morning he had filled forty buckets. But the more he thought about Skip and all the other things that had suddenly engrossed his life, the angrier he became. He stopped once and crushed a tomato in his hand, causing the juice to run down his arm like blood. Then he dumped the bucket on the ground and stomped the tomatoes into a pulp.

Cy came up beside him and said, "Mistuh Jay, you don't

need to be stompin' them 'maters. They don't belong to Creedy. They just belongs to somebody who's payin' to have 'em picked.''

Jared felt foolish. He said, "I guess you're right." Cy's words calmed him, and he tried to push the angry thoughts from his mind. But he did not stop the urgency of his pace. By noon his bucket had been dumped seventy times.

During the break they sat in the white dust and shared two cans of mackerel and a package of crackers. Cy came to them and said, "Mistuh Jay, you better take it easy. You goin' to kill yo'self. It don't matter none at all how many buckets you fill."

"I'm fine," Jared insisted. "I feel fine." He wiped sweat from his eyes and drank the juice from the mackerel can.

When they got back to the camp that afternoon, Jared went immediately to the van and discovered that Skip was missing. He searched around the camp but could not find the body or any trace of a fresh grave. Then he looked across the south field and saw that buzzards were circling the edge of the swamp. He cursed to himself as he walked back to the room.

Bennie met him at the door and said, "Are we goin' to bury Skip now, Papa?"

"Somebody has already done it. I could see the grave outside the fence." He did not want Bennie to know that Skip had been dumped at the edge of the swamp for the buzzards to eat.

"Did they bury him without words?" Bennie asked.

"I don't know. But we can say words fer him here in the room. Skip won't know the difference. We'll do it after supper."

Just after dark, Jared went out to the north fence and paced back and forth, trying to convince himself that things were not really as bad as they seemed. He thought that perhaps he was agitating for nothing. In two days he had picked two hundred and seventy-three buckets of tomatoes, and both Bennie and Kristy were doing better than they had done the previous week. If he could keep up this pace, he should be able to clear the debt in less than two weeks. Then they could either work the fields in another camp or move on somewhere else. Jared stopped the pacing and grabbed the fence with both his hands. He swayed back and forth as he was suddenly overwhelmed with tiredness. Then he walked unsteadily back to the room.

When he came inside, Bennie looked up from his bunk and said, "Papa, we ain't said the words yet for Skip."

Jared had forgotten all about this. He dropped to his knees on the concrete floor and said softly, "Lord . . . bless Skip . . . make a place fer him up there with some woods to roam and a few rabbits to run, and he'll be happy . . . take good care of him, Lord . . . that little dog didn't mean no harm to nobody . . . and Lord, watch over us all . . . ."

When he finished, he got up and fell wearily across his bunk, not even removing his clothes. He was asleep instantly.

EIGHT

ALL OF the words from Cy and the danger signals from his own body did not slow Jared's pace for the rest of the week. Each day he picked more tomatoes than the day before, and each night he was asleep before the orange sunset receded from the western sky. He did not even mind the slop they were fed for the evening meal. He chewed automatically and swallowed, too numb from fatigue to know or care what he was eating.

Cloma noticed this, and it troubled her deeply. She had never seen Jared act this way. He had always enjoyed his food and then sitting around after supper, discussing the events of the day and making trivial talk. Bennie and Kristy also noticed, but they knew the reason for his tiredness. They did not understand why their father was working at such a frantic pace, and they did not question him; but both were concerned as they watched him in the fields each day.

Saturday finally came. When the workday ended, and they reached the camp, Jared went to the room immediately and started figuring. He had picked eight hundred and fifty-two buckets for the week; Bennie had three hundred and six, and Kristy two hundred and forty. He added the figures slowly and carefully. The total of thirteen hundred and ninety-eight buckets was an earning of three hundred, forty-nine dollars and fifty cents. Then he figured the charges: forty dollars for rent, five dollars for electricity, fifty-six for the evening meals, thirty-six for the bus, eighteen dollars advanced for food, and ten dollars and fifty cents for the bottles of wine lining the wall. This came to one hundred and sixty-five dollars and fifty cents. He subtracted this from the earnings and it came to one hundred and eighty-four dollars. Then he remembered the ten dollars Creedy had advanced, and this reduced the amount of clear money to a hundred and seventy-four dollars. This, subtracted from the three hundred and seventy-two dollars and fifty cents that he owed Creedy, brought the debt down to one hundred and ninety-eight dollars and fifty cents.

He felt great relief. With a little more effort they could clear the debt the next week, and if they did not quite make it, he could pay the difference. All of the numbing tiredness suddenly rushed from his body, and his mood became jubilant. He jumped up and kissed Cloma on the forehead, and then he said, "Ev'rything's o.k.! We're goin' to be just fine!"

She gave him a questioning look, then he left the room quickly and joined the pay line.

When Jared reached the table, Creedy examined the ledger; then he looked up and said, "You did pretty good this week, Jay Bird. You've reduced your debt by fifty dollars. That brings the total down to three hundred and twenty-two dollars and fifty cents."

It took several moments for the words to register, and then Jared said angrily, "That ain't so, Mr. Creedy! We made a hundred and seventy-four dollars free and clear! I don't owe but one hundred, ninety-eight dollars and fifty cents! I figgered it myself!"

Creedy's face flushed. He said, "Goddammit, Teeter, I keep the books! You owe what I say you owe!"

Jared stepped back because of the sudden outburst. He looked Creedy directly in the eyes and said, "Mr. Creedy, I'll tell you what I'm goin' to do. I got a hundred and fifty dollars left from the trip down here. I'm goin' to give it to you. Then I'm goin' to get my family in my van and drive out of here. I'm goin' right through that gate and not look back, and you ain't goin' to stop me."

Creedy jumped up and shouted, "Nobody leaves Angel City owin' me money! Nobody! You understand me? You ain't goin' nowhere!"

Jared said calmly, "I'm goin' to drive through that gate and leave. And you ain't goin' to stop me."

Jared had not seen Jabbo standing behind him, and the blow was totally unexpected. He hit the ground on his stomach. He tried to push himself up but was too stunned to move. He lay still for a moment, waiting for his eyes to focus. There was a tremendous ringing in his ears, but he heard Creedy say, "Give him another one, Jabbo!" Then he felt the heavy brogan shoe crash into the side of his head.

Jared did not know how long he had been on the ground. When he finally pushed himself to a sitting position, the line of people was gone. Creedy was standing over him. He threw a ten-dollar bill to the ground and said, "Here's your advance for next week, Jay Bird." Then he turned and left.

The supper line had formed when Jared reached the hydrant beside the shower stall. He turned the water on and let it run over his head, then he walked slowly back to the room.

Cloma, Bennie and Kristy were waiting outside the door. Cloma said, "What took you so long, Jay? We'll miss supper if we don't hurry." She noticed that his head was wet and that his face was beginning to swell. "Jared, what have you been doing out there?" she asked with concern.

"Not anythin'," he answered. "I just stopped by the hydrant to wash up some. We can go to the supper line now."

They went to the cookshed and then returned with plates of food. Jared took only a few bites, then he put the plate down and said, "Cloma, I got a thing to say, and I want all of you to listen real good."

"What is it, Jared?" she asked anxiously, still puzzled and disturbed by his sudden change of mood.

"The gate is open fer the buses to go to the store. I want all of you to stand by the east end of the building. I'm goin' to go out to the van. When I crank it, all of you run and jump in. We're leavin' here."

"How come we're doing this all of a sudden? You told me before supper that ev'rything was goin' to be all right."

"Just do as I say!" he said harshly.

"What about our things here in the room?"

"Leave them! And go now!"

Jared walked to the van slowly. No one was around. He put the key into the ignition and pushed the starter. The engine remained silent. He eased out of the door and opened the hood. When he looked inside he saw immediately that the battery was missing. He closed the hood and walked back to the building.

"We better get on the bus and go to the store now," he said without emotion. "We'll need food fer next week."

Cloma was completely baffled by his actions. She did not understand any of this, and it was causing her great concern. Her thoughts were troubled as they joined the line of people pushing their way into the bus.

When they returned to the camp, Jared sat on the edge of his bunk, his arms draped dejectedly across his lap. His head ached, and the right side of his face had turned purple. Cloma knew that something bad had happened and that he did not wish to talk about it yet, so she remained silent and did not question him further as she mended a rip in his shirt. Kristy was sitting on her bunk making a pot-holder, and Bennie was outside somewhere.

Jared looked closely at Cloma. It seemed to him that her stomach was swelling more and more each day. She also looked very young to him, almost as young as that day in the past when he had purchased her box of fried chicken at the church social and then shared it with her at the picnic table. He remembered the day of their marriage and their first night together, then the long walks in the woods and talk of the life they would share together in the mountains at Teeter Ridge. It had been a hard life but one with many moments of happiness. He also remembered how Cloma had looked when she was carrying Kristy.

He then turned his gaze to Kristy, noticing how much she looked like Cloma at the same age. Her eyes were deep blue and filled with innocence. She could not see the things that he saw, could not comprehend the reality of their present life. It suddenly came to him just how dependent all of them were on him. Their lives were almost totally in his hands, and he could make of them whatever he wished, like a potter molding clay. The thought frightened him. It was a heavy responsibility for any man, but now he had made the weight of it even greater. He looked at them both again, and he knew they did not deserve to be here in this camp or in this dingy concrete room where he had brought them. He had turned into a very bad potter, and it saddened him to think of it. He then got up and went outside.

Cy was leaning against the wall, drinking whiskey from a quart bottle. Jared sat down beside him. Cy said, "I seen what they done to you. But what they done this time ain't nothin' at all when you know what they can do."

"It was enough," Jared said.

"You want a drink?"

"No thanks," Jared said. Then he muttered absently, "They's got to be a way."

Cy put the bottle on the ground and said, "Mistuh Jay, don't you do nothin' foolish. Just bide yo' time an' wait. Ain't nothin' goin' to help you none if you daid."

"They's gotta be a way," Jared repeated. "We could get word to the police or somebody. Somebody would help."

"You'd just be wastin' yo' time," Cy said. He picked up the bottle and drank again, and then he said, "Folks don't care 'bout people like us. We ain't nothin' to nobody. We jus' don't matter none at all. The sooner you learn this, the better off you goin' to be. You gotta take it like it is. If'n you don't, then you goin' to end up doin' somethin' bad you would have never done. This the way it's always goin' to be. You gotta take it like it is, an' fo'get all the rest."

"Is that what all these people have done?" Jared asked.

"That's what they done a long time ago. These folks is daid, Mistuh Jay. A man don't have to stop breathin' to be daid. They done had the life knocked outen them. They was born daid. All they doin' now is hangin' on and waitin' to be planted. If they can get a place to sleep, an' somethin' to et, an' a bottle of whuskey fo' Satteday night, then they don't mind the pain of it."

"They'll not defeat me!" Jared said, a determination in his voice. "Not ever! We's mountain folk!"

"Mountain folk don't mean nothin' at all down here," Cy said. "Don't you do nothin' foolish." He pushed the bottle toward Jared. "Why don't you have yo'self a snort? It would sho' do you good. I know yo' head is bound to be hurtin'."

Jared took the bottle and removed the cap. He took a deep drink and handed the bottle back to Cy. The warmth of the whiskey flowing down his throat felt good, and he could feel it easing the pain in his head. He said, "Thanks. I appreciate it." Then he went back into the room and lay on his bunk.

NINE

JARED DID not slacken his pace when he went into the fields the next Monday. He realized now what Cy had meant when he said it didn't really matter how many tomatoes he picked; but he was determined to try once again to reduce the debt by a large amount. He thought that Creedy just might give him full credit for what he and Kristy and Bennie earned if they all worked as hard as they could and he did not create further trouble. It would at least be worth trying, and there would be nothing for him to lose except energy.

It was just after the noon break on Wednesday when Jared noticed that the old man called Rude was acting even more peculiar than usual. He had been picking all morning in a row next to him, and the old man had been constantly singing the song about seeing Jesus in the tomato patch. This did not puzzle Jared, for Rude sang to himself most of the time; but then he started dumping his buckets of tomatoes on the ground instead of taking them to the truck. As fast as he picked a bucket full, he dumped them where he stood, then he moved on and dumped them again. He was leaving a solid trail of tomatoes between the two rows.

Cy came up to Rude once and said something to him, but the old man continued to sing and dump the tomatoes. A few minutes later he dropped the bucket and wandered off toward a line of Australian pines lining the farm road. Jared watched as Jabbo followed after Rude and then brought him back into the field; but as soon as Jabbo was gone, Rude wandered off again. Jared saw no more of Rude until they got on the bus to return to the camp.

It was after supper when Creedy and Jabbo came around the side of the building. Jared and Cy were sitting on the ground, talking. Cy was the first to see them coming, and he said to Jared, "Mistuh Jay, no matter what happens, don't you take no part in it. They ain't nothin' we can do."

Jared said, "I don't understand what you mean."

"You will in a minute," Cy said. "Just don't you have no part of it."

Creedy walked to the door and looked inside. Rude was sitting on his bunk, still singing. Jared watched curiously as Creedy went inside. The sound of the first blow was like someone smashing a bottle against the concrete floor.

At first the old man screamed, and then he started crying. Jared jumped to his feet as Cloma came running outside. Her voice trembled as she said, "What in God's name is happening in there?"

"Go back in the room!" Jared said to her harshly. "And don't come back out here 'til I say so!"

Cy stepped in front of him as Jared moved toward the door. He said, "I done tole you! They ain't nothin' we can do!"

"We can't just stand here and let them do that to the old man!" Jared said desperately. "They'll kill him if we don't help!"

"They ain't nothin' we can do!" Cy shouted again as he pushed Jared backward. "You want to get the same fo' yo'-

self fo' nothin'?"

Jared could see through a corner of the door as the old man put his hands to his head, trying vainly to ward off the blows. The pistol smashed into his face again and again. The more times he was struck, the harder he cried; and then with each blow he started shouting, "Jesus! Jesus!"

Creedy finally came from the room and started to walk away. Then suddenly he seemed to become angrier. He said to Jabbo, "That ain't enough! Go back in and give the old fool a few more licks!" He turned and walked away as Jabbo went back into the room and started pounding Rude again with the pistol.

As soon as Jabbo was gone, Jared rushed into the room. Rude was swaying back and forth, his head in his hands. He was moaning, "Oh Jesus . . . Oh Jesus . . . Oh Jesus . . ." He was covered with blood, and blood was splattered over the walls and floor.

Jared went to his room and said urgently to Cloma, "Get some rags. We need your help. And hurry!" Then he took a bucket and ran to the hydrant for water. When he returned, Cy helped him place the old man on a bunk.

Cloma tried to wash the blood from the old man's head, but it came back as fast as she wiped it away. She finally said, "He needs help badly. There's nothin' I can do for these wounds. We don't have medicine or bandages."

"We'll have to do the best we can," Jared said.

Cy looked again at the smashed head and said, "The pore ole fool was tetched, but he sho' knowed how to pick. They should 'a let him go out o' here a long time ago. Now he'll leave fo' sho'. He might 'a made it outen here if he hadden been so good at pickin'. That's why Creedy kept him in here and wouldn't let him go."

Rude finally stopped moaning and then lay still. Cloma put another wet rag on his forehead, and then she said, "All we can do for him is keep his head cool and watch him during the night. The blood is beginning to slow. Do either one of you know what he did to make them so mad at him?''

"He didn't do nothin'," Cy said. "He was jus' old an' wore out. He stayed in the fields too long."

Jared and Cy went outside and sat on the ground while Cloma remained in the room with Rude. Jared leaned back against the wall and said, "I've seen mean folk in my lifetime, but I ain't never seen nobody like Creedy. He ain't real."

"He's real," Cy said. "They's men like Creedy ev'rywhere. The woods is full of 'em. But you just now findin' it out."

"Back in West Virginny, they'd take a man like Creedy and hang him to the nearest tree," Jared said.

"They wouldn't nowhere I ever been," Cy replied.

Jared thought for a moment, and then he said, "I'm glad I ain't been where you been. I couldn't have stood it fer this long." He got up and moved toward his room. "I'm dead tired, and I'm goin' to bed now. If you need help with Rude later in the night, jus' let me know."

"He ain't likely to need no help," Cy said. "And at least he won't have to pick tomorrow."

Cloma was waiting anxiously the next afternoon when the buses returned from the fields. She ran to Jared and said, "I've been takin' care of that old man all day, but since noon I can't tell if he's breathin'."

Jared and Cy went straight to the room. Jared felt Rude's wrist, and then listened to his chest. He turned to Cy and said, "He's dead. I better go and tell somebody."

Ten minutes after Jared had spoken to Jabbo, the giant black man backed the red pickup to the door. He and Clug loaded Rude into the back of the truck, then they covered the body with a piece of canvas.

Jared watched as the truck went through the gate and raced along the dirt road leading to the highway. It was creating a dense cloud of white dust. He turned to Cy and said, "I wonder how they'll explain those wounds on Rude's head?"

"Explain to who?" Cy asked.

"To the people at the funeral home, and maybe the police."

"He ain't goin' to no funeral home," Cy said. "He's headed fo' the swamp."

"You mean they'll just take him out and bury him?" Jared asked doubtfully.

"Either that or dump him in a sinkhole. Rude ain't the first one to leave in that pickup. They's been others. An' it don't make no difference if'n you daid or alive when you leave, you ain't comin' back."

"You sure you ain't just stretchin' it a bit?" Jared asked, still doubtful.

Cy said, "Mistuh Jay, if'n they ever tries to put you in that pickup, you best fight like a wildcat. That ain't no truck; it's a hearse. If you ever get in that pickup, you ain't never comin' back."

He said it so simply that again Jared believed.

As the week passed, Jared's pace began to slacken. It was not intentional, and for a time he did not realize he was picking fewer tomatoes. It became difficult for him to concentrate on the work with so many thoughts clouding his mind. He wondered how he could have stood idly by and only watched what was in reality a murder. But then it was as Cy said; there was nothing he could do. It also saddened him that the old man had died so alone with apparently no one anywhere who cared. It was as if a mule had died instead of a man. He thought that everyone should have someone somewhere who cared. Even Skip had been mourned. It also frightened him that Creedy or Jabbo or Clug apparently thought no more of beating a man to death than they would think of going into a barnyard and killing a chicken for supper. Such men were totally alien to his upbringing and previous way of life, and he could not bring himself to now accept them and their actions as a natural way of this new life he had ventured into. He also did not want his children to be witnesses to such things.

Each time he realized he was filling fewer buckets, he doubled his efforts during the next hour; but then he would again fall into a mood of depression and lag behind the others. He did not notice the rocks or the dust or the heat or the hunger; and he was not aware that Jabbo was watching him constantly.

When Saturday ended, he figured their week's total of thirteen hundred and twenty buckets. This gave them three hundred and thirty dollars, and deducting the expenses, there was one hundred and sixty-five dollars and fifty cents left. He subtracted this from the three hundred and twenty-two dollars and fifty cents, and the debt was reduced to a hundred and fifty-seven dollars. But he felt no jubilation as he had the previous Saturday.

He joined the silent pay line, and when he reached the table, Creedy glanced briefly at the ledger and said, "You've reduced the debt by thirty-five dollars this week. You're down to two hundred and eighty-seven dollars and fifty cents now."

Jared felt no surge of anger, and he was surprised at himself for this. He did not even argue. He accepted the ten-dollar bill and walked back to the east end of the building. Then he watched as each man and woman took the five-dollar bill handed them and then went back to their rooms. When the ritual was ended, he walked back to Creedy and said, "Mr. Creedy, I want to talk to you fer a minute."

"What is it now?" Creedy asked impatiently.

"I'll give you my van fer the debt."

Creedy glanced briefly at the truck, and then he said, "That old thing ain't worth nothing."

Jared said, "I gave my pickup truck and five hundred dollars fer it before we left West Virginy, and I spent a lot of money on it comin' down here. It ought to be worth a heap more than the debt. You can have it and we'll call ev'rything square. Me and my folks can walk back to Homestead."

"You must think I'm crazy," Creedy said. "That ain't no good deal at all. It ain't my fault if you let some used-car salesman ram a shaft up your rear. I'll take the thing and sell it and put what I get on the debt. You want me to do that?"

"If that's all you'll do, yes." Jared handed him the keys; then he walked back to the building. He looked back around the corner and watched as Jabbo brought the battery from the trailer and put it into the van.

TEN

THERE WAS more chill at dawn as October passed into November, but the Florida days were just as humid. Soon now there would be snow in West Virginia, with logs to chop and deer to hunt. The trees would be bare and somber, and the fields would lie fallow and brown. The earth would be crusty beneath the step as white layers of frost blanketed the yards and the houses and the woods. The days would be shorter and the nights longer; the glowing logs in the fireplaces would send thin spirals of black smoke upward into the gray sky. The beds at night would be piled with thick layers of quilts. Jared sensed that Cloma and Kristy and Bennie were thinking of these things, although they never spoke of them.

There was no visual change of season in the tomato fields or in the surrounding areas. The Australian pines and the cabbage palms and the royal palms all stayed the same as they had been. The fruit trees did not drop their leaves and become bare, and the tomato plants did not turn brown and wither. Instead, the buses continued to dump their human cargoes into the fields each day; the trucks continued to rumble along narrow farm roads, transporting thousands of crates of tomatoes and beans and squash and okra to packing houses in Homestead and Florida City; the rocky fields continued producing the fruits and vegetables which filled the shelves of supermarkets in distant towns and cities, and were eaten by snowbound people who had no thoughts about the where and the how of fresh fruits and vegetables during the winter. These things just magically appeared in supermarkets and were taken for granted by snowbound people.

The days also did not change for the residents of Angel City. There were cans of sardines and Vienna sausage to be eaten before dawn; there was a bus ride to the fields, where ten hours of picking awaited them; there were cans of sardines and slabs of cheese to be eaten at noon; there were late afternoon stops at the Gater General Store to purchase more cans of sardines and Vienna sausage and cheese to be eaten the next day; there was wine to drink and then a hot supper; and there were the stifling, airless rooms at night, and whiskey on Saturday. There were also the occasional sounds of pistol butts cracking skulls. It was all a part of providing the tomatoes for salads and sandwiches to be eaten in New York and Boston and Chicago and Detroit and New Orleans and Minneapolis and Denver and Toronto.

Each day was the same to Jared Teeter as he waited anxiously to learn if Creedy had sold his 1960 Dodge van. It was now the end of another week, and he had not seen Creedy since he had given him the keys the previous Saturday. He felt sure the van would clear the debt, so he had discontinued the frantic pace he had endured the previous two weeks. He worked at a steady pace and averaged ninety buckets per day.

As Jared waited in the pay line, he wondered if Creedy

might possibly give him some cash for the van as well as clearing the debt. If he received even a small amount of money he could purchase an old clunker in Homestead that would do for transportation until he could afford something better.

When he reached the table, Creedy looked up at him and said, "You didn't hardly even break even with the picking this week. How come you to slow down so much?"

At first Jared didn't answer. He was more interested in the van than the picking, and he did not want to say anything that might make Creedy angry. He finally said apologetically, "I was tired, Mr. Creedy. But I didn't think I did too bad."

Creedy said, "Well, you better step up the pace again if you're ever going to work off this debt. I got fifty dollars for your van at a junkyard, so you're down to two hundred and thirty-seven dollars and fifty cents now."

For a moment Jared remained motionless. He felt the blood drain from his face and his hands tremble. He suddenly bellowed, "Shit fire, Creedy! What the hell you take me fer, a goddam idiot?"

The boom of his voice startled the people standing behind him, and they began to back away. Jabbo and Clug moved closer to Jared. Creedy pushed the chair from the table and started to get up.

Jared looked first to Creedy and then to Jabbo and Clug. He had an overpowering urge to smash something with his fists, to strike Creedy regardless of the price he would have to pay. For several moments he hesitated, his body frozen rigid with anger; and then he picked up the ten-dollar bill from the table and walked quickly toward the barracks.

During supper he did not speak to Cloma or Kristy or Bennie. Just before he boarded the bus for the store, he took three twenty-dollar bills from their savings. After making his purchases, he changed the twenties into ones and stuffed the thick roll of bills into his pocket.

When they returned to the camp, Jared asked Cy to step aside with him. The two men walked out to the north fence. Jared stepped close to Cy and said, "I want you to help me with somethin'."

"What's that, Mistuh Jay?" Cy asked apprehensively.

"I got a plan," Jared said. "I know how we can make Creedy pay ev'rybody what they got comin'."

"How's that?" Cy asked, eyeing Jared closely.

"We just won't work. If we refuse to work, then Creedy won't make anything. And he can't beat up ev'rybody in the camp."

"I don't get what you mean," Cy said.

"When we go to the field Monday morning, we refuse to leave the bus 'til Creedy pays ev'rybody fer this week's work."

Cy scratched his head. "These folks in here won't do that. They be's afraid."

"He can't beat up ev'rybody on the bus," Jared insisted.

"I guess he can't at that," Cy admitted. "But I just don't believe nobody will do it."

"Maybe I got somethin' here that might help persuade them," Jared said. He pulled the roll of bills from his pocket. "How many folks ride our bus ev'ry mornin', 'bout twenty-five or thirty?" he asked.

"Somethin' like that," Cy answered.

"We'll give each of 'em two dollars. We'll try it first with just our bus. If it works, then the other crew can do it too."

"I don't know, Mistuh Jay," Cy said doubtfully. "I just don't know 'bout this. Creedy'll get maddern hell fo' sho'. Ain't no tellin' what he'll do."

"He can't beat up ev'rybody on the bus," Jared said again. "And it's worth a try. We don't have nothin' to lose but my money. Will you give out the bills and tell ev'rybody what to do?"

"How come you wants me to give out the money?" Cy

asked, again becoming apprehensive.

"They'll probably listen to you quicker than me."

" 'Cause I's a nigger?"

"Yes," Jared answered simply. "You don't have to argue with anyone. Just hand out the money and tell them what to do. That's all. If they get off the bus Monday mornin', there's nothin' we can do 'bout it. But maybe they won't."

Cy took the rolls of bills reluctantly. He said nervously, "O.k., Mistuh Jay. I'll do it. But soon's I'm done, I'm goin' to drink that whole bottle o' whuskey as fast as I can. Ole Creedy'll get maddern hell."

Jared watched as Cy entered the first room on the west end of the building.

ELEVEN

NO ONE spoke to anyone else as the workers boarded the bus Monday morning, and the trip to the fields was made in silence. Jared wondered if his plan would work, but there was no clue on anyone's face as to what they intended to do. An air of gloom permeated the bus, and each person glanced suspiciously at the others.

When the bus reached the field, Jabbo parked it beside an Australian pine and got out. No one moved. For a moment Jabbo seemed puzzled, then he got back in and said, "Git offen the bus!"

Still nobody moved. Jared stood up and said, "Nobody works this mornin' 'til we get paid. And you can tell that to Creedy."

Jabbo seemed to be totally bewildered. He glared angrily at the workers for several minutes, and then he backed the bus from beneath the tree and into the edge of the field. Then he closed the windows, got out and shut the door.

Minutes turned into hours as the workers remained in their seats. By mid-morning, the sun had turned the bus into an oven. Jared wiped sweat from his face as he wondered how long these people would hold out. For the first time, he felt a closeness to others in the camp besides Cy. Perhaps they weren't all dead yet after all, he thought.

Noon came, and the heat became even more intense. There was no water to drink and no place to perform the necessary bodily functions. Some people were beginning to squirm; but still no one moved toward the door.

At mid-afternoon Creedy came to the field. He spoke briefly with Jabbo and then left. Jared watched the Mark IV as it disappeared down the farm road. He smiled briefly. He too was beginning to hurt badly, but he felt a strong comradeship with the others on the bus who were also suffering. Even Kristy and Bennie didn't complain, although they did not understand what was happening.

The workers got off the bus silently when it returned to the camp. Not one word had been spoken during the entire day except for the brief statement made by Jared. Everyone seemed to be more tired than they would have been if they had picked.

Jared and Cy were sitting on the ground outside the room when Creedy, Jabbo and Clug came around the side of the building. Creedy was in a trot. He stopped in front of Cy and said harshly, "What the hell you mean, nigger?"

Cy didn't move, and there was deep fear in his eyes. Before he could speak, Jared got up and said to Creedy, "He didn't have nothin' to do with it. It was me who made up the plan."

Creedy turned to Jared and said, "If it was you, how come it was this nigger who gave out the money?"

"I gave it to him and told him what to do," Jared said calmly.

Creedy snorted. "You mean to tell me that a white man gave a nigger a fistful of money and told him to give it to other niggers? I don't believe it!"

"Where else you think he could have gotten it?" Jared asked. "You sure don't pay him anythin'."

Creedy gave Jared a menacing look. He said, "Do you mean to tell me you want to take this nigger's whuppin' for him?"

"I'm tellin' you it wasn't his plan," Jared insisted. "It was mine. He didn't have nothin' to do with it."

Cy stepped up and said, "That ain't true, Mistuh Creedy. I been savin' that money fo' a long time. This white man didn't have nothin' to do with it. He didn't even know. It was us niggers who planned it."

"That's what I thought!" Creedy snapped, again turning his attention to Cy. "You better go with us out to the cook-shed."

Cy walked ahead of them as they turned the west corner of the building. Jared followed close behind, but Creedy wouldn't listen to anything he tried to say. When the little group reached the cookshed, Creedy rang the bell.

People came slowly from their rooms as Creedy continued ringing the bell. Many had stark terror in their eyes. When they were all assembled in front of him, Creedy said loudly, "They ain't going to be any supper tonight for no-body! And the buses ain't going to stop at the store again 'til Saturday! You can eat tomatoes in the field if you get hongry! And I want all of you to see what happens to any son of a bitch who causes trouble and won't work!"

Creedy turned suddenly and smashed his fist into Cy's mouth. Cy went to his knees, and Creedy kicked him in the stomach. He kicked him twice more, then he turned to Jabbo and said, "You and Clug can have him now. Give him one he'll remember."

Cy tried to get away as the two men pounded him with fists and feet. Jared's face turned ashen as he watched, and then he leaned forward and vomited into the dust.

The beating lasted until Cy lay still on the ground. When

it was over, all of the workers went silently to their rooms. Jabbo and Clug stood over the body for a moment, then they turned and walked back to the trailer.

Jared lifted Cy from the ground and placed him in a sitting position. He squatted in front of him and said, "Can you get up if I help you?"

"I can try," Cy answered feebly. Blood was flowing from his nose and mouth.

Cy got up slowly and put his arm around Jared's shoulder. They moved one step at a time around the corner of the building and to Cy's room. Cloma was waiting with water and rags. She bathed the blood from his face as Cy slumped on the edge of the bunk.

Jared said in a pleading tone, "Why'd you do this, Cy? Why? That should a' been me out there, not you."

Cy looked at Jared and said unsteadily, "It don't . . . matter none 'bout me . . . Mistuh Jay . . . you got a . . . family to look after. . . ."

Jared suddenly felt a bond with this black man he knew would be with him for the rest of his life. He put his hand on Cy's shoulder and said, "You didn't have to do this. I can take my own beatin's."

Cy managed a feeble smile. He said softly, "Don't you know . . . you can't kill a nigger . . . by beatin' him on the head . . . white man hit me once . . . wid a crowbar . . . an' it busted the bar . . . I'll be all right . . . Mistuh Jay. . . ."

Jared didn't know whether to laugh or cry. He said, "Do you want wine? We have some in the room."

"That would sho' be fine," Cy said, seeming to catch a second breath like a runner. "But I sho' would like to have me some whuskey 'bout now."

"I'll buy you two bottles Saturday night," Jared said quickly. "And we'll have eggs Sunday mornin'."

"That sounds mighty fine," Cy said. Then he lay back on the bunk and closed his eyes.

It was three days before Cy was strong enough to go into the fields again. Cloma looked after him during the day, and Jared brought tomatoes from the field for him to eat. They also shared with him their meager supply of sardines and Vienna sausage, which would have to last the rest of the week. It hurt Jared deeply that Cloma and Kristy and Bennie and all the other people in the camp were constantly hungry. He wished he had never tried the useless plan that had brought all this trouble to everyone; and he vowed he would never again do anything that created a risk to anyone other than himself.

Jared continued to pick at a slower pace and ignored Creedy's previous warning to produce more if he wanted to reduce the debt. He did not count the number of buckets he picked. He thought only of finding a way out of Angel City, and this one goal became an obsession which pushed all else from his mind. Rather than frightening him into submission, the witnessing of Cy's cruel beating had made him more determined than ever to take his family and leave.

That Saturday afternoon when he joined the pay line, he did not care if Creedy did or did not reduce the debt and he stared blankly as Creedy told him that he had only broken even again that week. He accepted the ten-dollar bill without protest, and went back to join Cloma and Kristy and Bennie at the supper line.

After the trip to the store, he and Cy sat on the ground outside the room. Both remained silent as the sun disappeared from the sky and darkness crept into the camp. Neither of them had said anything more about the trouble earlier that week, but each day Jared thought he detected a hatred toward him in the eyes of the other workers. He knew that it was he alone who had caused all of them to be denied food and the one daily pleasure of visiting the store each afternoon. This hostility toward him — real or imagined — saddened him greatly, for he had not meant to bring harm to any of them.

Jared finally broke the silence and said, "I've got another plan."

Cy looked at him with disbelief. He said, "Mistuh Jay, ain't you learned nuthin' yet? You best take 'nother look at my face."

"This won't involve anyone but me," Jared said quickly, still feeling deep guilt and sorrow for what had happened to Cy because of him. "But all this has got to come to an end. I'll put a stop to it next week."

Cy still couldn't believe what he was hearing. "What you goin' to do now?" he asked apprehensively. He did not really even want to hear the answer.

"I'll buy my way out of the gate, then I'll go to Homestead and bring back the police. This thing has got to stop. It can't go on forever."

Cy shook his head. He said, "You goin' to fool around an' get yo'self hurt real bad. Creedy ain't playin'. You ought to know that by now."

Jared ignored the remark. He said, "It won't involve anyone but me. I'll go to Homestead and bring back the police."

Cy took a deep drink from his bottle. He wiped his mouth and said, "Are you sho' you know what you doin'? They's other folks in here 'sides you."

"I know that," Jared said. "And this time I won't bring trouble to them. But they're all in the same trap I'm in."

Cy pushed himself back against the wall. His eyes were troubled. He fumbled with the bottle for a moment, and then he said, "If these folks gets outen here, where they goin' to go? To another camp?"

"At least they'll have a choice," Jared replied.

"They ain't got no choice noways. The camps is all the

same. Only diff'rence 'tween Angel City an' any other is that the gate's locked here an' they ain't as much money to buy whuskey.''

"I'm not sure what you're sayin' to me," Jared said. He looked again at Cy's battered, expressionless face. "Are you tryin' to tell me that all these people in here want to live this way?"

Cy said, "I ain't sure myself what I'm tryin' to say. I'm just a dumb nigger, an' I knows it. But these folks is diff'rent from you, just like you an' me is diff'rent. You come in here 'cause you wanted to. Nobody made you. Us folks was born in the camps. It's all we knows, an' we ain't got no place else to go even if we wanted to. An' one camp's the same as another. But I just ain't sho' 'bout nothin' no more."

Jared gave Cy a penetrating look. "Do you want to stay here the rest of your life?" he asked. "Or do you want out, like me?"

For a moment Cy didn't seem sure of his answer. He seemed to be weighing the question. He finally said, "I wants out. But it's 'cause o' the boy. I wants somethin' better fo' the boy."

Jared also became silent for a moment, then he said to Cy, "How come you think I want out of here so bad? You think it's just fer me?"

A sudden understanding came into Cy's eyes. He said, "No. I knows now, an' I shoulda knowed all along. It ain't fo' you."

Both of them gazed into the darkness for several minutes, and then Jared spoke as if saying the words to himself, "It won't involve nobody but me."

Cy took another deep drink from the bottle and muttered, "I sho' hope you knows what you doin'."

TWELVE

IT WAS Wednesday afternoon just after supper when Jared approached Jabbo out by the trailer. Jabbo was eating a Moon Pie and sucking the chocolate from his fingers. He eyed Jared with distrust.

At first Jared just stared at Jabbo, and then he said hesitantly, "Can I talk to you fer a minute?"

"Whut you want?" Jabbo asked harshly.

Jabbo's tone made Jared reluctant, and he asked cautiously, "How'd you like to make some money?"

Jared watched the giant black man's reaction closely.

"Doin' whut?"

"Nothin' much. It would be worth fifty dollars to you."

Jabbo appeared interested. He said in a guarded tone, "Whut you want me to do?"

"Just open the gate tonight and let me out. My woman's feelin' poorly, and I need to go to the store real bad and get some stuff fer her. You let me out, nobody will ever know you did it, and I'll come back real soon."

"You got the money?" Jabbo asked.

Jared reached into his pocket and pulled out a wad of crumpled bills. He handed them to Jabbo and said, "Fifty dollars."

Jabbo took the money and put it into his pocket. He said, "Whut time you want to go?"

"As soon as it gets dark."

Jabbo wheeled suddenly and went into the trailer.

For a moment Jared stared after him, wondering if Jabbo would really open the gate or if he had given his money away for nothing. He knew that if Jabbo kept the money and left the gate locked, there was nothing he could do about it. But he was willing to take the risk.

He went back to the barracks and sat on the ground outside the room. He had said nothing of this to Cloma, for he knew she would be frightened by the danger involved and would try to persuade him not to do it, and he had not told Cy when he intended to put this plan into action.

Cy came back outside and sat beside him. For a few minutes they made trivial talk, but Jared was completely detached from everything except the approaching darkness. Cy noticed this, and wondered about it. Always before, Jared had seemed to enjoy their conversation as the camp settled into the night; but now, for all the attention he was paying to Cy's remarks, Cy might as well have not been there at all.

Jared did not speak to Cloma or even look into the room when he got up and walked slowly toward the east end of the building. The moon had not yet arisen, and the fields outside the fence were seas of darkness. He could not see the fence or the gate as he skirted the edge of the yellow cone being cast outward by the floodlight. His heart pounded as he moved past the clump of Australian pines.

When he reached the fence, he stopped and let his eyes adjust to the darkness. Then he pushed his body against the gate. It opened. He stepped outside and closed the gate behind him.

For a moment he looked back and searched the area around the gate. When he detected no sign of movement, he turned and started along the dirt road. He had an overpowering urge to break and run, but he knew he must not allow his footsteps to shatter the quietness of the fields and echo back into the camp. He moved slowly and carefully, one step at a time, feeling his way along the powdery trail as would a blind man. He looked back only once, and it seemed to him that the floodlit buildings were a thousand miles away.

Just as he reached a point forty yards from the highway, the truck's headlights came on and centered on him. The unexpected shafts of brilliant light blinded him, and he tried to shield his eyes. He heard the roar of the engine as it came to life, and then he heard the screech of tires. He realized vaguely that the pickup was moving directly toward him. For a moment he was unable to control his body; then at the last possible second he jumped aside as the truck rushed past him and skidded around wildly, once again bathing him in the blinding headlights.

Jared felt terror invade every part of his body as the pickup rushed at him again. He turned and ran into the field to his right. The truck also turned and came at him again. He stumbled as the limbs of the tomato plants grabbed at his legs; and when he tried to break free of them, the pickup started circling him. It did not come directly at him again until he ran blindly toward the south end of the field.

Each time the headlights seemed certain to smash into him, he managed to jump to the side; and then the game began again. He ran and circled and dodged and fell and then ran again; but no matter what he did, he could not escape the menacing beams of light.

He had reached almost total exhaustion when he felt the sharp sawgrass cut into his legs. He fell forward and landed in soft muck that splattered across his face. For a moment he lay still, panting and unable to breathe, then he looked back just as the headlights were turned off. He did not realize until then that the truck had been herding him into the marsh.

For several minutes more he did not move. There was no sound coming from anywhere except a bellowing off to his right. He had never before heard such a sound, and then he remembered what Cy had said about the alligators. The total darkness addled him, and he could not tell from which direction he had stumbled into the swamp.

He finally pushed himself up and staggered forward, but with each step he took, he sank deeper and deeper into muck and water. He could hear swishing sounds as snakes scurried out of his path. When the water level reached his chest, he turned and moved in the direction he thought he had come. The water gradually became shallow again, and then he was suddenly back in the edge of the field.

He sank down to the rocky soil and breathed deeply. About a mile to the west he could see the dim lights of the camp. After he rested for a few minutes, he got up and headed east across the field. He had moved only a few yards when the headlights came on and once again centered on him. He felt he did not have the strength left to even try, but he started staggering through the tomato plants.

The truck came at him again and again as he ran and stumbled and fell and ran again, and then he realized that the game was ended. If he continued to run they would kill him, so he dropped to the ground and lay still.

He heard the door swing open as the truck stopped ten yards from him, then he heard the rush of feet. The first blow stunned him as the pistol smashed against his face. He was surprised that it caused so little pain, and he did not put up his hands to ward off the blows. He was too exhausted to care what they did to him, and it was a relief when he felt consciousness slip away.

The jolt of his body hitting the floor of the truck bed aroused him, and he heard Clug say, "We goin' to take him to the sinkhole?"

"Naw," Jabbo's voice came to him. "Mistuh Creedy say bring him back to the camp. We goin' to take the girl."

Blackness closed in on him again, and he knew nothing more until he hit the ground outside his room. He felt himself being pulled inside and thrown on the bunk, and he had a twilight realization that Cloma and Kristy and Bennie were crying hysterically; but he could not force words from his mouth.

Jared looked up and discovered that he could see and hear, but he could not move or speak. He listened as Jabbo grabbed Kristy by the arm and said, "Mistuh Creedy say fo' you to come to his place."

He heard Kristy scream, "No! No, Papa! I'm afraid! I don't want to go, Papa! I'm afraid!"

Jared tried with all that was left in his body to push himself up, but he could not do so. He watched helplessly as Jabbo dragged Kristy to the door.

Cy suddenly stepped out of the darkness and said, "Why don't you two niggers leave that girl alone? Is Creedy payin' you that much? You done enough to her pa already."

"You want some too," Jabbo asked, his eyes glazed with hostility.

"I'd as soon as not!" Cy shot back angrily. "You goin' to give it to me by yo'self, without no help from Clug? You try it by yo'self, I'm goin' to beat tha' livin' shit outen you."

Jabbo stepped toward Cy, dragging Kristy with him, then he stopped and said, "I'll settle wid you later. We gotta take the girl now."

Cy watched Kristy struggle as Jabbo pulled her to the pickup; then he stepped into the room and said to Cloma, "Is Mistuh Jay hurt bad?"

"I don't know," Cloma sobbed. "Oh my God, I just don't know!"

Cy went to the bunk and examined Jared's face and head.

Then he turned to Cloma and said, "I don't think he's got nothin' broke, but they sho' whupped up on him real good. Ain't no need fo' you to fret so. He'll git all right in a few days, an' I'll help look after him."

Cloma sat on the edge of the bunk and bathed Jared's head. She said to Cy, "What did he do?"

"He snuck out fo' Homestead," Cy answered. "I tried to tell him, but he wouldn't listen. He thought it were a game. I tried to tell him these folks ain't playin'."

THIRTEEN

THE NEXT morning when he awoke, Jared could hardly push himself from the bunk. Both of his eyes were almost swollen shut, and he had a purple welt down the right side of his face. The muscles in his arms and legs ached each time he moved, and sharp pains shot through his ribs where he had been kicked.

He took the coffee Cloma handed him and sipped it slowly. At first he did not remember the events of the previous night, then they started coming back to him like fragments of a dream. He could see Kristy being dragged from the room, and the thought of her being held as a prisoner by Creedy made him sick. He put the coffee mug on the floor and pushed it away.

For several minutes he sat on the edge of the bunk, trying to put all of the pieces together in his mind. He knew now that what Cy had said was true: this was no game. Each day since he had learned the harsh reality about Angel City, he had hoped that it was all a bad dream that would fade away, that he would awake one morning and find it did not exist at all; but he knew from the empty bunk where Kristy had been, and the pains in his own body, that this was not to be. His situation was totally beyond his understanding, but it was a deadly serious reality.

Jared got up and forced himself outside when the bell rang for the loading of the buses. Cloma pleaded with him to remain in bed, and Cy cautioned him not to go to the fields, but he paid no heed to either of them. He was determined at any cost to show Creedy that he had not been beaten into something less than a man. Walking slowly and painfully one step at a time, he reached the bus and climbed aboard.

There were times that day when Jared could not remember filling the bucket or taking it to the truck. His eyes were narrow slits, and he picked by feel rather than sight. As the heat became more intense, his head pounded beyond endurance; and several times he dropped to his knees and vomited into the green plants. It was mid-afternoon when he finally sank to the ground between the rows and did not move again until Bennie and Cy helped him to the bus at the end of the day.

Each day for the rest of the week, Jared went back into the fields, and gradually his strength began to return. On Saturday afternoon, when he reached the pay table, he glared defiantly at Creedy as he was handed the ten-dollar bill.

Before going to the store, Jared took ten dollars from the sixty dollars left of his savings, and after making his food purchases, he bought two quarts of whiskey. Cloma watched the precious money change hands but said nothing. She knew what he felt he must do.

Late that afternoon, Jared sat on the ground outside the room, a bottle on each side of him. He had already taken several drinks when Cy came out and sat beside him. Cy opened his own bottle, then he said to Jared, "It looks like you plannin' a party tonight."

"I thought I'd do some drinkin'," Jared replied, not fully

aware of what Cy had said.

"Don't blame you none," Cy said. "Man take a whuppin' like you did, an' then go back to the fields, he oughta drink some. You the most stubborn white man I ever seen."

Jared turned the bottle up and drained it three inches, then he said, "Folks is killin' hawgs now in West Virginny." He was trying to flush the present from his mind and submerge himself into the past, but the mountains and streams seemed to be too far away, if they ever existed at all.

Cy said, "I sho' would like to have me a big ole fresh ham an' some baked sweet taters. I could et a ham as big as a watermelon."

"We made our own hams and bacon and sausage and lard," Jared said, drinking deeply again. "Smoked the meat with hickory. I always liked to put a piece of fried sausage between a hot biscuit. We had real butter too, and in the winter there was deer meat."

Cy said, "Mistuh Jay, you oughta hush up. You makin' that salt poke an' stewed squash we et fo' supper swish aroun' in my belly. I's gittin' hongry just listenin' to you. How come you to up an' leave all them good vittles an' come down here?"

Jared drank again, and then he said, "Well, I didn't rightly want to, and when we finally pulled up stakes and shucked out for Floridy, I was scared spitless. Times just got too hard in the mountains, and I couldn't make it no more. Taxes was too high, and they wasn't much way a man could make cash money. I cut logs on one of my ridges 'til they ran out, and I hauled some firewood. Two winters I left home and worked in the coal mines, but I couldn't stand it down there under the ground. The Lord didn't mean fer a man to burrow around like a mole and then die with that black stuff in his lungs."

"I wouldn't like that neither," Cy said. "I just got to have me some fresh air all the time."

Jared turned up the half-full bottle and drained it in one gulp. Then he threw the empty bottle toward the fence and opened another. Cy watched him curiously and said, "You oughta take it kind of easy, Mistuh Jay. They's plenty of the night left ahead o' us."

Jared turned to him and said sharply, "Goddamit, you think I don't know how to drink?"

"I didn't mean nothin' at all," Cy said quickly, startled by Jared's angry response.

"Folks aroun' Dink make they own whuskey," Jared said, his voice now as calm as if he had not made the previous remark to Cy. "It's a heap better'n this store-bought stuff. When it comes outen the still it's white, but you put it in a charcoal keg and it turns brown."

For a moment Jared fell silent, then he turned back to Cy and said, "You ever do any coon huntin'?"

"I done some once up in Georgie," Cy answered.

"We used to go ev'ry chance we'd get," Jared said. "Went mostly just to hear the dogs run. Go out in the woods and build a fire. Never did mess with the coons, though. But I had a uncle who did. His name sounded almost like my wife's. It was Clomer. He always got drunk before the hunt started, and when ev'rybody else was just sittin' round the fire, listenin' and talkin', Uncle Clomer would run after the dogs and go up in a tree after the coon. He'd catch one and then bring him back to the fire and turn him loose so's the dogs would run after him again. One night Uncle Clomer went up in a tree, and he was really shirt-tailed drunk. He grabbed that coon by the rear legs and started jerkin'. Only it wadden no coon. It was a wildcat. But Uncle Clomer was too drunk to tell the diff'rence. At first the wildcat thought Uncle Clomer wanted to play, so he gives Uncle Clomer three or four quick jabs with them big back feet. Kicked just like a mule. But Uncle Clomer didn't turn loose. Then that ole cat commences to get mad. He started makin' a nest in Uncle

Clomer's hair, only he was takin' it all off Uncle Clomer's
head. It sounded like they was tearin' the whole top out of
that tree. Leaves and branches was flyin' ev'rywhere. Then
the wildcat decided he'd take off Uncle Clomer's ears, but
Uncle Clomer had other plans. He just couldn't understand
why a coon would carry on so. About then Uncle Clomer
gets mad too. In a few minutes we heard the damndest
whump you ever heard, so we all run over to the tree, and
there on the ground . . ."

Jared suddenly stopped talking, leaned back against the
wall and took another deep drink. When he said nothing
more, Cy asked anxiously, "Well, Mistuh Jay, what happened
to yo' Uncle Clomer?"

Jared remained silent for several more moments, his eyes
transfixed on something past the fence and the fields; then he
finally turned to Cy and said, "I ain't a nobody! I was a
deacon in the church! I had a cousin who was a town alder-
man in Mudfork. I ain't a dried cow turd you can stomp on
and kick!"

Cy couldn't understand Jared's sudden shift of conversation, and was confused as to how to respond to it. He said
hesitantly, "I knows you ain't no cow turd, Mistuh Jay. I can
tell you's fine folks."

Jared drank again, and then he said softly, "Oughta be
snow soon in West Virginny. Kristy was born durin' a snow.
I got the pickup stuck and had to fetch the doctor on a mule.
I was a heap more scared than Cloma. She just laughed at me
after it was over. And that baby was so little. She looked just
like a doll. Never did cry much. I'd pick her up and bounce
her up and down on my knees. She really liked that. She
would coo just like a pigeon. Never did really cry much. She
was a good baby and . . ."

Cy watched as tears welled in Jared's eyes. He put his
hand on Jared's shoulder and said, "Mistuh Jay, you needen'
fret so. Yo' girl goin' be all right. They ain't done nothin' to

my boy since he been over there. She goin' be all right, Mistuh Jay."

"They's a diff'rence," Jared said, "a heap o' diff'rence. That girl never been away from home even one night before we came here. She ain't been aroun' like your boy, and she won't know how to handle it. And besides that, they's a big diff'rence 'tween a boy and a girl. You oughta know that."

Cy wanted to say something that might help ease Jared's fear, but he could not do so. He merely repeated, "She goin' be all right, Mistuh Jay."

Jared turned up the bottle, drained it half-way and started singing, "Wes - Vir - Ginny . . . mountain mamma . . . take me home . . . where I belong . . . Wes - Vir - Ginny . . . mountain mamma . . . country roads . . . take me home . . ."

Suddenly he pushed himself up and staggered unsteadily to the north fence. He laced his fingers through the heavy wire and shook the fence violently, then he dropped to his knees and said, "I ain't never done nothin' really bad in my lifetime, Lord . . . not a really bad thing . . . but You better help me now, Lord . . . You better help . . ."

Jared fell forward and lay still against the fence. He was not aware when Cy picked him up and carried him back to the room.

FOURTEEN

ON SUNDAY, Jared's moods changed constantly from anger to depression, and he moped around the compound like someone in a trance. Cloma tried to talk to him and cheer him, but she couldn't get through to him no matter what she said. When the Mark IV pulled into the camp and parked by the trailer, Jared ran to it anxiously. Kristy was not with the other children, and this caused him great fear. For the rest of the afternoon, he sat by the north fence alone, staring across the field and at the highway leading to Homestead.

The next day Jared picked the tomatoes automatically, filling the bucket and emptying it and filling it again. At noon he ate a can of sardines and a tomato, but the chewed pulp stuck in his throat. He spat the tomato to the ground and washed his mouth with water.

When he walked into the store at the end of the day, he appeared to be calm. After purchasing food he handed the sack to Bennie, then he walked to the store manager and said loudly, "You got to help us! We're prisoners! You got to help us!"

Jabbo moved toward him immediately. The store manager backed away and said, "You must 'a got too much sun, fellow. You better sit down and rest for awhile." Then he turned aside and waited on another customer.

Jared backed toward the door, repeating loudly, "You got to help! . . . somebody has to help!. . . ."

When he reached the front of the store, he turned right and ran up the highway. A car approached from the west, and Jared jumped in front of it, waving his arms wildly. The car swerved to avoid hitting him, then it increased speed. He ran again until he reached a house a quarter-mile up the highway, then he crossed the yard and knocked on the front door. When a woman opened it, he said urgently, "You got to help us . . . we need help . . . somebody has to help . . ." The woman slammed the door quickly and locked it.

Jared then looked down the highway and saw that Jabbo was coming after him. For a moment his senses were overcome with panic, then he jumped from the porch and ran into an orange grove to the south of the house. It was dark when he finally stopped running and paused for a few minutes beneath a papaya tree. After pulling one of the gourd-like fruits and sucking the juice, he wandered again for another hour until he dropped to the ground exhausted and fell asleep.

The sun was already mid-way in the morning sky when Jared awoke. He sprang to his feet startled and bewildered, not knowing where he was or how he got there. As reality gradually drifted back to him, he looked around and saw that he had spent the night at the edge of a bean field. Far in the distance he could see men and women picking into hampers. He knew that if he turned north again, he would eventually come back to the highway.

When he reached the road leading to Florida City, he dared not walk along its edge for fear that Jabbo or Clug would be looking for him; so he stayed behind houses and in the fields and groves until the outskirts of town came into view. At the first service station he came to, he asked directions to the police station.

It was another two miles to the Homestead branch of the sheriff's department, and as Jared walked along the roadway and sidewalks, people stared at his torn, filthy clothes and his battered face. He glanced around constantly to see if he was being followed. When he reached the small brown stucco building he went inside quickly.

The first room was a small lobby area, and as Jared entered, a man behind a desk eyed him suspiciously. "Something I can do for you?" he asked quizzically.

"We need help," Jared answered quickly. "We're bein' held against our will, and they've taken my daughter. Somebody has to help us."

The man gave Jared another penetrating look as he said, "Just have a seat over there and Deputy Drummond will talk to you in a few minutes. I'm just a clerk."

Jared waited nervously for ten minutes until finally he was asked to step inside an office. As he took a seat in front of the desk, an officer said, "I'm Deputy Drummond. What's your problem?"

Jared spoke rapidly, "We're bein' held like slaves! . . . . They've taken my daughter! . . . . You got to help us! . . . ."

"Just take it easy, fellow," the deputy interrupted. "Calm down a bit. Are you a migrant?"

"I work in the fields," Jared replied, trying to calm himself. "We came here from West Virginny."

"What's your name?"

"Jared Teeter. Folks call me Jay."

For a moment the deputy toyed with a pencil on the desk, then he looked back to Jared and said, "Just tell me the truth, Mr. Teeter. Have you been shooting junk or drinking too much wine? You could save us both a lot of time if you tell me the truth.''

Jared was surprised by the question, and he answered firmly, "I ain't been doin' nothin' like that! We need help real bad.''

The deputy looked closely at Jared's condition and said, "O.k. Now who is it that's doing all this to you?''

"His name's Creedy. Silas Creedy. We live at Angel City.''

"I've never heard of either one of them. But we don't keep track too much of the migrant camps. There's just too many of them.''

Again the deputy studied Jared closely. "Just exactly what is this man Creedy doing to you?'' he asked.

"He keeps us in the camp and won't pay nobody,'' Jared said, trying to think of all the things he should say. "Claims we all owe him money and we got to stay there and work it out. Can't nobody get outside the camp. I tried to get out and go fer help, but they caught me and then they took my girl off to Creedy's place as a prisoner. He's got the other folks' children there too.''

"Where does Creedy live?'' the deputy asked.

"I don't know,'' Jared replied, troubled by not knowing, for he wanted to go there immediately. "I guess it's sommers around here or Floridy City, or maybe in Miami. And it could be out in the country sommers.''

"That's not much help,'' the deputy muttered. He then said, "How'd your face get so beat up?''

"They pistol-whupped me,'' Jared said, wincing as the memories came back. "They beat one old man to death that way, then they took him into a swamp to get rid of him. I seen it. My friend's been in Angel City two years. He says they've killed a whole bunch of folks and put them into a sinkhole.''

The deputy thought for a moment, trying to digest all of the things Jared was saying. "That's a pretty bad story, Mr. Teeter,'' he said. "How far is it to this Angel City camp?''

"I can't rightly say fer sure," Jared answered, "but I can show you the way. It's not too fer out of Floridy City."

From Jared's straightforward answers, his simple sincerity and the urgency in his voice, the deputy surmised there must be some truth in the things Jared had said. He got up from the desk and said, "Maybe we might better go out to this Angel City and take a look."

Jared followed the officer outside, then they got into a green patrol car with a red flasher on its top. As they drove into Florida City, the officer turned to Jared and said, "How long's it been since you've eaten anything?"

Until then Jared had not even thought of food. He said, "I don't rightly remember. It must be nigh on two days now."

The deputy stopped at a hamburger stand and bought Jared two hamburgers and a milk shake, and he wolfed them down eagerly as they passed through the town and turned west on the highway leading to the camp.

It was after six when the patrol car turned from the highway and crossed the field to the camp. To Jared's surprise, the gate was open. The deputy parked beside the trailer and got out.

Creedy came from the trailer immediately, approached the deputy and said calmly, "I see you got ole Teeter. He's kinda daffy, if you ain't found it out already."

The deputy ignored Creedy's remark about Jared and said, "Are you Creedy?"

"That's right," Creedy answered. "I'm the contractor who runs this camp."

"Mr. Teeter here has told me some pretty bad things about you," the deputy said, watching Creedy closely.

"I done already told you he's tetched. I do everything I can to look out for him, but sometimes he goes plumb loco and runs off. You can ask his family about him."

"Mr. Teeter says you're holding his daughter and some other children at your house. Is this true?"

Creedy began shuffling his feet. "I ain't never heard such a wild tale," he said indignantly. "I live right here in the trailer. You can look for yourself."

Jared had been standing to the side, listening. He turned to the deputy and said, "That's a lie! Jabbo and Clug live in the trailer! Creedy don't live here at all!"

The deputy looked at the flash of anger in Jared's eyes, then he turned back to Creedy. "You mind if I have a look around?" he asked.

"Suit yourself," Creedy said, his voice unconcerned. "Look all you want to."

As the deputy went into the trailer, Creedy turned to Jared and said in hushed tones, "If anything comes of this, you're in bad trouble. You must 'a forgot where your girl's at."

Jared was worried, for he had not expected things to go as they were. He had surmised that the deputy would simply arrest Creedy and then return Kristy to him. But he still thought that the officer would surely learn the truth before leaving the camp. Thus far he had only heard Creedy's side of the story, and he knew that Cloma and Cy would tell the truth.

When the deputy came back outside, he said to Creedy, "I'll look around the camp for a while. You wait here until I return."

Jared followed the deputy as he went to the first room on the north side of the building. He looked inside and said, "You folks got anything to say to me?"

Four somber black faces stared back. One said, "Naw suh."

"Can you leave this camp if you want to?" he then asked.

"Yas suh. We can leave anytime we wants."

Jared's face was ashen as he listened to the unexpected answers.

The deputy moved on down the line and received the

same reply in each room, then he came to Jared's room. Cloma was sitting on one bunk and Bennie on another. She looked at Jared and said, "Where've you been, Jared? We've been worried sick about you."

Before Jared could speak, the deputy asked, "Is this your husband?"

"Yes," Cloma answered calmly. "That's Jared."

"Where's your daughter?" he then asked.

"We don't have a daughter." Cloma stared downward, avoiding Jared's eyes. "We only got Bennie here."

Jared's heart sank, and he knew now why the gate had been open instead of locked. Creedy had had ample time to prepare the camp. Jared was not surprised when Cy told the deputy he had no son.

After questioning several more people, the deputy walked back to the trailer with Jared following. He leaned against the side of the patrol car, staring intensely at Creedy, then he said casually, "That's a mighty fancy car for a labor contractor."

Creedy looked toward the Mark IV and said defensively, "I earned ev'ry penny of it. I works hard. I go into the fields ev'ry day and picks right alongside my people."

The deputy was unimpressed by Creedy's remarks. "How come this man's face is so beat up?" he asked, studying Creedy's reaction.

"How would I know?" Creedy snorted. "He ran around in the woods all last night. Maybe he fell over something. I try to take good care of him, but sometimes he goes plumb loco."

The deputy sensed that Creedy and all the others were lying, but he couldn't take the word of one man against all the others in the camp. He turned to Jared and said, "I guess I'll be going now, Mr. Teeter."

"Ain't you goin' to arrest him?" Jared asked feebly.

"For what?" the deputy said. "Nobody here will back up

your story, not even your wife."

"I told you he's tetched," Creedy said, now feeling confident.

"Maybe he is and maybe he isn't," the deputy snapped, looking directly into Creedy's eyes. "I can't prove anything now, but this whole place don't look right. How come you've got it fenced like a prison compound?"

"Too much thievin' goin' on," Creedy said warily. "You know how it is with these migrants wandering around all over the countryside. They'll take anything that ain't nailed down. And besides that, it ain't against no law to put a fence around your own property."

When he reached the patrol car, the deputy turned and said, "You take it easy, Mr. Teeter. And Creedy, I might be seeing you again."

Jared watched the patrol car as it turned through the gate and moved toward the highway, taking with it his one hope of getting Kristy back and escaping from Angel City. As he walked dejectedly toward the barracks, Creedy shouted, "Hold up there, Teeter!"

Creedy came to him and said, "We ain't goin' to whup you this time, 'cause it don't seem to do no good. But you owe me a fair and honest debt, and you're goin' to pay it one way or another. You pull another stunt like this, or cause trouble of any kind, and that gal of yourn might have a real bad accident. You understand what I'm saying, Jay Bird?"

"I understand," Jared said, his face and voice strained with defeat. "I ain't goin' to cause no more trouble. I swear it."

Creedy was pleased by Jared's answer. He said, "It's about time you figured it out. I ain't never had nobody come in here before who acted like you over an honest debt. From now on, you get only four dollars on Saturday instead of what I been givin' you. If your belly starts to hurt, it ought to make your brains work better."

"My wife needs plenty of food," Jared said, concerned by Creedy's remark about the money. "Her time's not too far off, and she needs to keep up her strength. Do what you want to me, but don't punish her fer what I done. She had nothin' to do with it, and she needs her strength."

"You ought to have thought about all that before," Creedy said. "If your woman gets hungry, you can give her part of your vittles from now on."

"I'll do that," Jared said as he turned quickly and walked away.

When he entered the room, Cloma grabbed his arm and cried, "I'm sorry, Jared! I'm sorry! I ain't never lied before, and you know it. But Mr. Creedy said he'd hurt Kristy real bad if I didn't do as he said. And he threatened Cy and all them other folks, too. I'm real truly honest sorry, Jared, but I didn't know what else to do! I was afraid for Kristy!"

"I understand," Jared said, looking deeply into her eyes as he took her into his arms and tried to calm her. "It's all right. I know you couldn't do nothin' else but what you did. It's all right, Cloma, don't fret about it. You done the right thing."

Two days later, late in the afternoon, Creedy entered the camp with a drunken black man sitting beside him in the Mark IV. The man got out and staggered around the side of the building. When he came to where Jared and Cy were sitting on the ground, he said, "Is this room 'leben? Mistuh Creedy say I'm in room 'leben. I's goin' work fo' Mistuh Creedy."

"You found it," Cy said.

The man had a brown paper sack in his hand. He said, "I's called Hoot, an' I comes from Orlando. Mistuh Creedy, he let me have ten dollars in advance. He a good man. He goin' pay me twenty-five cents a bucket fo' pickin' 'maters."

Cy pointed into the room and said, "You got the bunk on the right. The man what had it befo' you had to leave here a short while ago. Just go on in an' make yo'self at home."

Hoot went inside for a moment, then he came back out and said, "You folks wants a drink? Mistuh Creedy, he give me this here whole quart bottle o' whuskey."

"Don't mind if I do," Cy said, eyeing the bottle. "You can sit down here on the ground an' join us fo' a spell, a good long spell. We sits out here ev'ry afternoon after supper."

FIFTEEN

DAYS MERGED into each other as the buses left the camp each morning before dawn and returned in late afternoon. The routine was broken twice when the workers were shifted from tomato fields into bean fields; and for three other days they planted tomatoes instead of picking them. They did not know what they were being paid as planters, and the money Creedy gave them each week remained the same.

When the month changed to December, the daylight hours were shorter, and sometimes the light did not come until a half-hour after they entered the fields. Dusk settled before supper was finished, and the wind at night was strong and piercing. Flights of ducks and geese passed overhead as they headed out into the vast marshlands of the Everglades. Rain came more often, and sometimes the ground inside the camp turned into a quagmire that sucked at shoes and covered the concrete floors of the rooms.

Since Kristy was no longer in the fields, Jared received only two dollars each day for food, and this, combined with the four dollars he received on Saturdays, gave him sixteen dollars each week for food and all the other necessities. He ate less and gave Cloma and Bennie more, and at night he bathed without soap in order to divert every possible penny into additional cans of sardines and Vienna sausage. He brought tomatoes from the fields, and sometimes he would slip from the fields into adjoining orange groves and steal fruit, which he brought back to the camp in a brown paper sack he kept inside his shirt. He also asked the store manager for waste beef and pork bones, which he boiled into broth each night and left for Cloma to drink during the day.

Kristy came for visits on Sunday afternoons, and each visit they saw a change in her personality. The constant smile she once wore was now gone, and she showed little interest in anything. Jared tried to question her about how she was being treated, but she would not answer. Instead, she would turn and walk away alone, ignoring his pleading calls for her to come back and be with the family. Sometimes she would stand for hours clinging to the fence, gazing out across the empty fields; and when it came time to leave the camp, she would walk away without saying goodbye to any of them. This caused both Jared and Cloma great anguish and concern, but there was nothing they could do but hope that the change was only temporary.

Jared made no further plans for escape. Instead, he decided to do as Cy suggested and bide his time, waiting for something unexpected to come from some unknown somewhere and set him free. He wanted to get out of Angel City as badly as ever, but his spirit was shattered, and he was determined to do nothing more so long as Kristy remained outside the camp, and so long as his actions might endanger her life. Each day was lived as it came, and his life slipped into a routine just as regimented and drab and as accepted as that known by any of the workers who had spent lifetimes in the camps.

He began to think and feel and act more as Cy did. Sometimes he hated himself for letting his life become so totally controlled and guided by Creedy. When he became angry enough because of this, he would share Cy's bottle of whiskey on Saturday nights. He would look forward to those few hours on Sunday afternoons when all of his family could be together, although most of the time Kristy was not with them at all; then on Monday mornings he would go into the fields and lose all conception of hours and days until another weekend came again.

It was on a Saturday night that Jabbo came down the line of rooms on the north side of the barracks. Jared and Cy were sitting on the ground outside Cy's room, and they were immersed in darkness except for a narrow shaft of light drifting through the partially closed door. Hoot was inside, passed out on his bunk. Jabbo suddenly appeared out of the shadows and said, "Mistuh Creedy say fo' you to be on the bus at six in the mornin'."

"What fer?" Jared asked harshly, startled and annoyed by Jabbo's unexpected presence on a Saturday night. "We ain't never picked on Sunday."

"Mistuh Creedy say we takin' one bus full o' men to work in Belle Glade fo' awhile. He say all men on the north side be on the bus at six."

It took a moment for the meaning of Jabbo's words to register on Jared, and when they did, Jared said, "I ain't goin' to do it! I'm not leavin' this camp with my wife the way she is!"

Jabbo repeated, "Mistuh Creedy say fo' you to be on the bus at six. An' you leave the boy. We ain't takin' nothin' but men on the bus." Then he walked on down the line of rooms.

Jared turned to Cy and said, "What's this all about? How come they'd take us to Belle Glade?"

"To pick," Cy said, without surprise or concern because

of the sudden order. "Up there they grows sweet corn an' celery an' lettuce. He might even put us in the sugar cane fields. If he puts us in them cane fields, then you sho' goin' need you a bottle ev'ry night."

"I thought we stayed here all the time. Creedy didn't tell me nothin' about goin' some place else."

"We goes where they's work," Cy said. "Beans an' cukes in Carolina, peaches in Georgie, 'taters in Alabam, oranges anywhere he wants us to go. If them buses wadden so old an' rattly, we'd go up to Noo Yawk an' pick grapes an' apples, but Creedy ain't goin' spend the money to fix 'em up to go that far."

Jared became silent for a moment, "I ain't goin' to go! They'll have to drag me on that bus feet first an' kickin'!"

Cy shook his head with exasperation and said, "I thought you'd done learnt better. You don't go, all you goin' do is make things worse fo' yo'self an' bring on a heap o' trouble fo' yo' girl."

Jared realized that again Cy was right. He asked, "How long will we be gone?"

"It's hard to say. Depends on the crops an' how many folks is already workin' up there. Most times it's two-three weeks or a month, but the crops lasts all winter up there. Could be a long time, but sometimes the pickin' gets better down here, an' he brings us back. We follow the crops anywhere they points that old bus."

"I can't leave Cloma that long, the baby is due soon."

"They ain't nothin' you can do 'cepin' get yo' head bashed in or yo' girl in trouble. That wouldn't help yo' woman none, would it?"

"Maybe Creedy would let Kristy come back to the camp and stay with her."

"They's a woman called Bertha in the other side of the buildin'. She's a midwife, an' she's a good woman, too. I'll speak to her 'bout lookin' out fo' yo' wife."

"What if she needs a doctor?" Jared asked.

"She won't get no doctor even if you's here. An' you knows that. I'll go speak to Bertha."

Cy got up and went around the side of the building.

Before he went in to tell Cloma, Jared decided that he would see if Creedy was still in the camp. He walked to the trailer, and the Mark IV was there. When he knocked on the door, Creedy came out.

Jared said, "Mr. Creedy, will you bring my girl back to the camp when we leave for Belle Glade tomorrow?"

"What for?" Creedy asked.

"My wife's expectin' soon. Kristy could look out fer her while I'm gone."

"You must think I'm crazy!" Creedy snapped. "I wouldn't let you go four feet outside the gate with that girl back here. You'd probably shuck out for West Virginia."

"Let her come back to the camp," Jared pleaded. "If you do, I swear 'fore God I won't do nothin'. I ain't caused no trouble lately. Let her come back, Mr. Creedy."

For a moment Creedy seemed hesitant, then he said, "I ain't going to do it! You got a boy to look after your woman. You ought not to have gotten her belly swelled up like that noway. She ain't been to the fields a day since she's been here."

"Who'll be here if she needs help?" Jared asked, realizing that Creedy would never grant his request.

"Clug is stayin' here with the south crew. While ev'rybody's in the fields, the cook will be here during the day. Ain't that enough? And besides that, they's some nigger women who can help out. Hell, them nigger women knows how to handle it. They has babies out in the fields, then goes on picking the rest of the day."

Jared knew it was useless even talking to Creedy. Without speaking further, he turned and walked back to the room. He dreaded telling Cloma.

SIXTEEN

CLOMA AND Bennie walked with him as Jared answered the bell to board the bus. To Jared the shrill clanging seemed to be an ominous forewarning of impending doom. It was as if some pagan temple bell were tolling him away so that his wife and unborn child could be sacrificed to a god of the fields he could not accept or comprehend. He wanted desperately not to go, to stay and share with Cloma the agony and joy of this thing they had created together, this intimate moment of love they had shared in the past which would soon produce life. He knew this desire was hopeless, so he consoled himself with the thought that perhaps he would return to Angel City before the time of the birth.

When they reached the bus, he kissed Cloma and cautioned Bennie to look after her as best he could; then he turned away from them quickly and stepped into the dark interior of the old vehicle. As they passed through the gate and moved slowly along the dirt road, he looked back and could see Cloma and Bennie standing alone beneath the floodlight on the east end of the building.

The sky was overcast that morning, and dawn did not come until they reached the northern outskirts of Homestead. Jared looked through the grimy window and watched the houses and the vegetable stands and the fields flow by. The fields were now empty and forlorn, resting until the next day when hordes of pickers would swarm over them like locusts.

A few miles north of Homestead, Jared thought he recognized the spot beside the highway where they had stopped to let the van's radiator cool on the day they arrived in Homestead. He remembered the lunch of sausage and crackers and hot Coke, and the conversations about the fruit stand and the ocean and fishing and bathing suits and things to come. He knew now that all those dreams they had talked about were only dreams, and they had been washed away like a sandcastle in a mountain stream.

They soon passed the junction of Highway 27 and the Tamiami Trail, and continued north on Highway 27. Jared passed the time by looking out of the window constantly, watching the people and the cars and the houses and the groves and the vast stretches of sawgrass at places where the Everglades swooped in and touched the edge of the highway. He also saw migrant camps which were in even worse condition than Angel City, rotten wooden shacks on stilts and unpainted concrete block barracks with bare yards and naked children and junked cars and trash and beer cans and people with hopeless faces looking out of broken windows, watching the flow of traffic along the highway.

When they reached Andytown, a light rain was falling, and the sky far in the north was a solid wall of black. "Cold front movin' in," Cy said to Jared. "It rain hard 'nough we won't be able to pick, then ole Creedy'll blow out his flue fo' sho'."

For several miles north of Andytown the highway cut through another section of the Everglades; then they reached the beginning of the vast areas of the sugar cane farms, fields of solid cane that stretched to and beyond the horizon and dwarfed even the largest tomato fields Jared had seen around Angel City. He looked in wonder at the soil, which was as black as thick layers of soot, and was puzzled by smoke boiling upwards from walls of fire stretching across the land.

Cy watched Jared with amusement, then he said, "They burnin' the cane fields befo' the cane's cut. Burns off the leaves an' trash. Most o' the cane's cut by voodoo niggers."

"What's voodoo niggers?" Jared questioned.

"Niggers from the islands. Pickers won't cut no cane lessen they ain't nothin' nowhere to pick an' they has to. It's too hard work. But them men they brings here from down at Jamaica swings them heavy machetes like they was made o' paper. You ain't never seen nothin' like how them niggers can go down a row o' cane."

Jared continued to stare at the endless fields. He asked, "You ever cut any?"

"I done it some, but I sho' don't like to. I'd ruther pick a thousand buckets of 'maters than spend a day in the cane."

"I don't see how they ever get it all chopped," Jared said.

"You would if you knowed how many men they puts out there in them fields at one time. All you can see is voodoo niggers swingin' them big blades."

It was just before noon when the old bus ambled into South Bay. Here the highway skirted the south shore of Lake Okeechobee. To the left were Bean City and Lake Harbor and Clewiston and Moore Haven; to the right, Belle Glade and Pahokee. The bus turned to the right.

Two miles out of South Bay the bus left the highway and followed a dirt road flanking a drainage canal on the right and a cane field on the left. A mile down the road they came to a clump of Australian pines. Just as Jabbo parked the bus beneath the trees, a solid sheet of rain poured down on them.

The pounding rain lasted for more than two hours, and

the men sat in the bus in silence. No mention was made of food, and Jared's stomach rumbled as he wondered when they would be given something to eat. When the rain finally stopped, they got off the bus and wandered around the small area beneath the trees.

It was late in the afternoon when the Mark IV pulled up beside the bus. Creedy got out and had a lengthy conversation with Jabbo. He opened the trunk of the car, took out a cardboard box and sat it on the ground; then he got back into the car and drove off.

The box contained cans of sardines and beans and loaves of white bread. Jabbo gave each man a can of each and two slices of bread. Jared and Cy sat on a bed of wet pine needles and ate from the cans with their fingers. Jared said, "Where'll we stay tonight? Does Creedy have a camp up here too?"

"We in his camp now," Cy said, drinking the oil from the sardine can. "You can sleep on the ground or in the bus."

There was no water except that in the nearby drainage canal, and it was covered with green slime and had a foul odor. Jared drank just enough to wash the food down his throat.

Some of the men gathered wet firewood which they coaxed into burning, but the wet wood produced more smoke than warmth. The temperature dropped rapidly as the wind became stronger and made a mournful wailing sound as it rushed through the thick limbs of the pines. Jared went into the bus and got a blanket he had brought with him. He draped it around his shoulders and sat as close to the weak fire as possible, but even this didn't help. His body shivered with cold as he got up and went back into the bus, and finally he fell asleep on the seat with Cy huddled close against him.

SEVENTEEN

DAWN WAS far off when Jabbo awoke the men the next morning. He again gave them cans of sardines and beans and slices of bread, but there was no coffee to ease the biting chill. During the night, the temperature had dropped into the mid-thirties. Jared had not brought even a light jacket with him, for he had no prior knowledge of the cold fronts that rush through Florida in the winter, dropping the temperature forty degrees overnight.

The meal was finished quickly, and then the workers were ordered into the bus. Just as they turned right on the highway toward Belle Glade, a feeble dawn revealed a steel-gray sky. Two miles down the highway they again turned onto a dirt road flanking a cane field. Cy looked out of the window and moaned, "Ah, crap! We ain't headin' to the corn fields. They must be too wet. He's takin' us to a cane field."

Jared didn't know the difference between a vegetable field and a cane field except for the remarks Cy had made about cane cutting, so he made no reply to Cy's seemingly disturbed remark.

When the bus stopped, Jared noticed that the Mark IV was parked beside a pickup truck. Creedy was talking to a man in the truck. All of the men were then ordered off the bus, and Jared shivered with cold as the piercing wind bit into his body.

Another truck was parked nearby, and a man at that truck issued each of the workers a machete and assigned him a row of cane. For those like Jared, who had never cut before, he demonstrated that the cane must be cut at ground level and then cut again into four-foot lengths. Jared gripped the handle of the huge blade and swished it through the air. The weight of it caused his arm to drop, and he almost sliced the blade into his leg.

The first hour of cutting was a novelty to Jared, and he swung the blade back and forth vigorously, striking down the hard stalks, cutting them again and throwing the lengths to the ground for the automatic loaders to scoop up. Soot from the burned stalks covered his face and arms and got into his eyes, and the black muck sucked at his shoes; but still the uniqueness of the work made the first of the morning bearable.

By noon his arms and back and legs ached almost beyond endurance, and the machete became heavier and heavier. It took all his strength just to lift the blade after he had swung it downward into the base of a stalk. He stopped almost continuously to rest, and each time he looked up, the row seemed to grow longer and longer. When the work was finished that afternoon, Cy had to push him back into the bus.

That night they again ate the cold food from cans and drank in the drainage canal. Jared managed to wash some of the grime from his face and arms, but his clothes were caked with thick layers of mud and soot. He made a bed of pine needles and then rolled himself into his blanket. He was so tired he didn't notice the cold or the dampness of the ground or the wailing sound of the wind in the pines, and it was just after dusk when he fell into a deep sleep.

The temperature dropped again to twenty-nine degrees, and even the constant swinging of the heavy machete did not warm Jared's body. His hands shook as he chopped again and again at the thick stalks, and at noon he huddled against Cy in the bus to gain some warmth. He wished that Jabbo would pass out the bottles of wine at night as he had at Angel City, for this might help bring some relief from the cold and the ache in his bones.

It was late in the afternoon on the fourth day in the cane fields when the pickup followed the bus back to the camp in the Australian pines. The emblem of a sugar company was painted on the doors of the pickup, and a tall radio antenna was mounted on the truck's cab.

A man got out of the pickup and looked at the ANGEL CITY sign on the side of the old bus, then he walked to Jabbo and said, "Is this the crew run by a man named Creedy?"

"Yassah, this it," Jabbo replied.

"You people been camping here all week?" the man asked.

"That's right," Jabbo said. "This our camp."

"Creedy stay here too?"

"Nawsuh. He stay at the motel in Belle Glade. He be out here soon with the food."

The man went back and sat in the truck until the Mark IV drove in and parked by the bus. He watched as Creedy put the box on the ground and Jabbo issued each man the cans of food and slices of bread; then he walked over to Creedy and said, "You Creedy, the contractor with this crew?"

"That's right," Creedy answered. "What you want?"

"I'm one of the field supervisors with the sugar company, and you're camping in my section. How long you had these men here?"

"Since Sunday," Creedy said warily.

"Are they sleeping on the ground?"

"They can sleep in the bus if they want to."

"It's a damned wonder they all don't have pneumonia." The man watched the workers as they sat on the pine needles and ate with their fingers from the cans. He said, "I've never seen a crew that looked worse than this. When's the last time these men had a bath?"

"I don't know nothin' about their personal habits," Creedy said, becoming agitated by the questions. "They can take a bath in the canal anytime they want to. Hell, I ain't no nursemaid. I'm a contractor."

"They can't stay out here any longer," the man said. "You can move them into a barracks at Camp 9."

"What's that going to cost?" Creedy asked.

"We'll give them the same deal as the offshore workers. The rooms are free, and the meals are seventy-five cents each."

Creedy thought for a moment, and then he said, "I ain't going to pay no two and a quarter a day per man just for meals. I can feed 'em myself for less than a buck."

"What do you mean, you're not going to pay?" the man questioned. "The meals are deducted from the men's wages. It has nothing to do with you."

"I get all the money and I pay the men," Creedy said firmly.

"What?" The man gave Creedy a penetrating look, then he said, "There's no way you're going to do that! We'll pay you the same as any contractor for putting these men in the field, but every man receives his own wages."

"I ain't going to do that!" Creedy said defiantly. "I get the money and I pay the men. Some of these people owe me money, and I have to take it out of their wages."

"You got a court order to do that?"

"A court order? Hell, I don't need no court order to collect a honest debt."

"You do up here." The man stepped closer to Creedy and said, "Fellow, I don't know what kind of an outfit you're running wherever you come from, but these men look worse than a bunch of pigs. Are you going to move them into the barracks or not?"

"Before I do, I'll take 'em out of the field!"

"You just do that!" the man snapped angrily. "And you get the hell off this property! You're on company property without permission! You're trespassing!"

"We got some money coming," Creedy said quickly.

"I know that. I'm going over to the field office and see exactly how much each of these men have earned. Then I'll come back and pay them. I'll be gone about a half-hour." He walked to the pickup, got in and drove off quickly, spraying mud from beneath the truck's rear wheels onto the side of the bus.

As soon as the truck was gone, Creedy kicked the cardboard box violently, scattering cans across the small clearing. He shouted loudly, "Bastards! Sons o' bitches! A man can't even make a honest livin' no more on account of them supervisors!"

The men sitting beneath the trees watched curiously as Creedy kicked the box again and again until finally it landed in the drainage canal.

When the supervisor returned, each man was given an envelope with his wages inside. The workers were paid according to the amount of cane each had cut, and Jared's envelope contained fifty-two dollars. He stuffed the bills into his pocket. Creedy stood to the side and glared angrily as the supervisor finished his task and got back into the pickup. He leaned out the window and said to Creedy, "I want you off this property within thirty minutes! And I don't want to ever see you back!"

Creedy watched the truck until it disappeared into the growing darkness, then he turned to the men and said, "I'm going to be fair with all of you. I got expenses bringing you up here, and the food. I'll let you keep half what the man gave you, and I'll take half. That's more'n you got comin'. And I'll let the bus stop at a store when we leave here."

Each man got up silently and walked to Creedy, handing him half the money he had received. Creedy stuffed the bills into a brown paper sack and then took Jabbo aside. They talked for several minutes, then Creedy got into the Mark IV and drove off. At Jabbo's signal, the men gathered up their blankets and boarded the bus.

When they reached the highway they turned right and drove to Belle Glade, then they turned north toward Pahokee. A mile out of town the bus stopped at a country store. The men scrambled out and rushed into the building, hurriedly purchasing cartons of beer and bottles of wine and Moon pies and jars of pickled pigs' feet and boxes of sugar cookies. Jared bought a denim jacket for eight dollars, several cans of corned beef and sardines, a quart of red wine, and two candy bars. He thought immediately of Cloma and Bennie back at Angel City without enough food, but he was too cold and too hungry to resist spending this much of the unexpected money. He still had over fifteen dollars left.

They drove north again for two miles, then the bus turned from the highway and followed a dirt path to an abandoned labor camp. The wooden cabins contained about nine square feet of space each and were propped on stilts four feet off the ground. The windows and doors were missing from all of them, and some of the cabins had gaping holes in their sides and roofs.

Jabbo cut the engine and said, "Mistuh Creedy say we stay here fo' a while."

Jared and Cy entered one of the cabins cautiously. They

were immediately covered with cobwebs, and the rotten floor sagged with their weight. There was a strong smell of decay. Cy said, "It ain't much, but it's better'n the ground. Makes me kinda homesick, too. Let's look aroun' an' see if we can find somethin' to build a fire in."

They went outside and searched the area surrounding the cabin. Jared found a rusted bucket half buried in the dirt, and Cy gathered a bundle of twigs. A few minutes later, a small fire inside the bucket illuminated the interior of the cabin. Both men held their hands over the flames to warm them.

Jared and Cy both opened cans of corned beef, then they drank deeply from bottles of wine. Cy said, "It sho' did me good to see that sugar man give it to Creedy. I thought ole Creedy was goin' choke to death on his own spit."

"Where'll he take us now?" Jared asked between bites.

Cy swallowed a huge chunk of corned beef, washed it down with wine, and then said, "Mos' anywhere. Probably the corn fields, but he sho' ain't goin' to take us back to the cane fields. Them folks don't want no more truck with Creedy."

"Suits me fine," Jared said. "I don't never want to cut another stalk noways." He spread out his blanket and lay down. The wine warmed him, and the new jacket felt good to his arms and shoulders. "How long these cold spells last?" he asked. "I always thought it was hot all the time in Floridy."

Cy drank again, then he put the bottle down and said, "Sometimes it gets cold enough to freeze the oranges on the trees, an' they has to fire the groves. But these spells don't last long. This one last much longer, the vegetables be in real trouble."

"I wouldn't care if ev'rything froze solid tonight. Maybe then we would go back to Angel City."

"You's worried 'bout yo' woman, ain't you?"

"Yes." Jared had not realized it showed so much on his

face and in his voice.

Cy said, "You don't need to worry so. Bertha a good woman. She'll see to yo' wife. Bertha will take good care o' her."

"Maybe," Jared said doubtfully. "But I sure wish I was back there now."

EIGHTEEN

IT WAS after ten the next morning when Creedy arrived at the camp. He passed out the cans of food, then he said impatiently, "You men can eat on the bus. We're runnin' late."

The workers boarded the bus hurriedly, and Jabbo followed the Mark IV back to Belle Glade and then east on Highway 441. Five miles out of town they pulled to the edge of a sweet corn field and stopped. A driver was waiting in a flat-bed truck piled high with empty crates. As soon as the bus was emptied, the workers followed the truck into the field, pulling the ears from the stalks and packing them into crates, then loading the crates on the truck and starting again with empty crates. When the truck was loaded, another took its place, and the loaded truck headed back to the packing house in Belle Glade, where the corn would be pre-chilled and then packed into other trucks to be shipped to markets in the East and the Mid-West and Canada and the Far West.

After work that day they returned to the abandoned camp for the night, and the next day they picked in the same field. It was Saturday, but when Creedy came to the camp late that afternoon, he did not hand out any money. Jared didn't really expect to receive any, since he had been allowed to keep half the money he earned in the cane fields, which was more than several weeks' pay at Angel City. The other men in the crew didn't seem to be concerned one way or another. They took the cans of sardines and beans and went back into the dilapidated shacks.

Jared and Cy sat on the floor of the cabin, eating in silence. Jared was glad there would be no trip to a store that afternoon. He still had some degree of pride left within him, and he was ashamed of the way he looked. Grime and soot were ground into his face and hands, and his clothes were stiff with caked dirt. He longed for a bath even if in a slimy drainage canal, but it was still too cold to risk such exposure.

They had not finished eating when Jabbo came to the cabin and ordered them outside. As they got up, Jared said, "We must be goin' to move again. Maybe it's back to Angel City this time."

Creedy was standing at the front of the bus, his red face flushed even redder with anger. When all the men were outside, he said, "We got a nigger missing. The one called Hoot. Who knows about it?"

The men glanced around at each other, but no one spoke. Creedy walked to the Mark IV and returned with a bottle. He said, "I'll give this quart of whiskey to the first man who tells me where the bastard went."

The group remained silent for several moments, then an old man of about sixty-five spoke up and said, "I seen him, Mistuh Creedy. Right after we got to the camp I seen him runnin' t'ward the highway. I seen him, Mistuh Creedy."

"Which way did he go when he got to the highway?"

"I don't know, suh. I couldn't tell fo' the trees. But I seen him runnin' t'ward the highway."

Creedy turned to Jabbo. "He couldn't have gotten far by now." Then he handed the bottle to Jabbo and said, "Put this back in the car. I ain't givin' away a quart of whiskey for no more information than that."

The old man stepped back into the group and cast his face downward.

Creedy then said, "I want you two men over there to go with Jabbo to Pahokee, and you two there to go with me to Belle Glade. The rest of you stay here at the camp, and you damned well better be here when we get back, or we'll be out lookin' for you next. You understand me?"

The men nodded their heads silently.

The first two men Creedy pointed to were Jared and Cy. All of those he selected to leave the camp and help search for Hoot were ones whose children were at his house.

Jared and Cy followed Jabbo to the bus as Creedy and the two men left in the Mark IV. When the bus reached the highway it turned right and followed the narrow highway which wound past cane and vegetable fields and was bordered on both sides by thick lines of Australian pines.

Darkness was flooding the highway as they arrived at the southern outskirts of Pahokee. This was the Negro section of the town, and on each side of the road, two-story concrete-block apartment buildings were jammed one against another. Some had once been painted in garish colors of pink and red and yellow which were now faded badly. All of them looked as if a stiff wind would send them tumbling down one against another like a line of dominoes. Clothes hung from sagging wooden balconies, and the yards were bare of grass and littered with trash and with rusted junk cars without wheels, propped up on wooden blocks.

Jabbo pulled onto a side street, parked the bus and motioned for Jared and Cy to get out. He said, "You two work the west side an' I'll take the east. If'n you find him, bring him back to the bus."

Jared and Cy walked together for a block. Silent men were huddled against walls and squatting along the sidewalk, some drinking beer and wine and whiskey, and others just looking and spitting into the street.

As they stopped beneath a dim street light, Cy said, "I'll work this side an' you work over in the next block. We'll meet down at the south end."

Jared touched Cy's arm and said, "What you goin' to do with Hoot if you find him?"

"I'm goin' tell him to run like hell an' never look back."

Jared smiled. "That's what I thought."

As Jared turned to cross the street, Cy said, "You best be real careful around here. This a bad part o' town." Then they walked in different directions.

Jared paused on the next corner and watched the people move about and the flow of traffic along the street. He was not aware of the police car's presence until it pulled to the curb beside him and stopped. An officer got out and came over to him.

Jared became apprehensive as the officer stared closely at his physical appearance. Finally the officer said, "What are you doing here, fellow?"

For a moment the situation addled Jared, and then he said, "I'm just walkin' around some."

"You a migrant?" the officer asked.

"I work in the corn fields. We live in a camp just south of here."

"What company's camp?"

Jared hesitated again, then he said, "I don't know the name of the company. We work for a contractor. He brought us into town in the bus."

"Is it the red bus parked on the side street over yonder?" the officer asked, pointing across the street.

"Yes, that's the one. We're just spendin' a while in town. We'll go back to the camp pretty soon."

The officer looked closely at Jared again and said, "You ain't got no business in nigger town on Saturday night. Don't you know that?"

"No, sir, I didn't know," Jared said nervously. "I was just walkin' around some."

"Well, you better walk in another area. We have enough trouble as it is without you just plain asking for more."

Jared felt relieved as the officer got back into the patrol car and drove away. He thought of the night he had so desperately wanted to talk to a police officer, and now he had lied to get rid of one. But he knew that if the police in Homestead wouldn't believe him, an officer in Pahokee would probably think him even crazier. And he was also thinking of Kristy.

As he walked along the street he could feel eyes following him, and finally he turned into a place called the Pastime Cafe. There was a counter along one end of the room, tables jammed along the sides and center, and a constantly flashing Budweiser sign on one wall. The air smelled heavily of smoke and fried fish and onions and hamburgers.

Several black men and women were sitting at the tables, and a fat black woman of about forty was behind the counter. When Jared walked to the counter and leaned against it, the woman gave him a hostile look and said, "What you want, mister? This is nigger town. You ain't got no business in here."

Jared was startled by the anger in the woman's voice. He said, "I'm lookin' fer a man called Hoot. He's a black man, 'bout my age, six feet tall and about a hundred and fifty pounds. Have you seen him tonight?"

"I seen a hundred like him," the woman said, becoming even more sullen. "What you want with him?"

"I need to talk to him. Has he been in here?"

"You want to buy somethin'? If you don't want to buy somethin', why don't you just get the hell on out o' here?"

"I'm just lookin' fer Hoot," Jared tried to explain again.

A man at a table by the counter had been watching and listening. He got up and came over to Jared. Suddenly he pulled a knife from his pocket, touched a button and a six-inch blade swished out. He pointed the knife at Jared and said, "Why don't you quit pesterin' her? You tryin' to start trouble? You lookin' fo' trouble, then you come to the right place."

Jared eyed the knife and the hostility in the man's face. He said as calmly as possible, "I'm not lookin' fer trouble. I just need to find a man called Hoot. I got to talk to him and help him out."

"I ought to drop yo' guts on the flo'!" the man said, moving closer as Jared backed away. Others in the room stopped drinking and watched.

Jared backed against the wall and kept his eyes on the glint of the knife blade. He was totally bewildered, not understanding what he had said to cause such trouble. He wanted to run, but now the man had moved between him and the door.

Jared glanced to the side just as Cy entered, and relief flashed through him at the sight of Cy's muscled body. For a moment Cy froze, and then he said loudly, "Hold up there, fellow! That white man's a friend o' mine!"

The man turned and stared at Cy. For a moment he hesitated, then he folded the knife and put it back into his pocket. He said to Cy, "If he's a friend of yourn, then you tell him to keep his damned mouth shut an' stop askin' questions in here!" Then he turned and walked back to his table.

Cy said to Jared, "We better get on outen here now. You just lucky I came in when I did. That fellow looked like he was 'bout ready to make bacon outen you."

They went outside and stood by the curb. Jared's hands were trembling as he said, "I sure don't know what that was all about. All I did was ask if they'd seen Hoot."

"It's best you fo'get it," Cy said. "But we better stay

together from now on."

They continued down the street and came to a building
with a sign on the outside: BEER AND POOL. When they
entered, Hoot was standing at a counter alone, drinking a
bottle of beer. Cy went to him immediately and said, "What
the hell you doin' in here? Don't you know Creedy's out
lookin' fo' you? He's got folks here an' in Belle Glade."

Hoot wheeled around in surprise. He said, "I wadden
runnin' away. I swear fo' God I wadden. I just wanted to
come into town an' get me a beer. I was comin' back."

"You crazy nigger fool!" Cy snapped harshly. "Don't
you know Creedy's just as liable to kill you as not?"

"I swear fo' God I wadden runnin' away," Hoot said
again, his eyes bulging with fear. "You goin' take me back
now?"

"We ain't takin' you nowhere," Cy said, his voice calmer.
"But you better hide sommers the rest of the night an' then
shuck out o' here as fast as you can in the mornin'. You can
go up to Avon Park or Frostproof. They's plenty of work
there in the groves, an' Creedy won't find you. An' you
better not ever come aroun' Homestead or here again."

"I can't get away lessen I gets back on the road an'
catches a ride," Hoot said desperately. "I ain't got a cent left.
Mistuh Creedy he goin' find me fo' sho'."

Jared reached into his pocket, took out a ten-dollar bill,
handed it to Hoot and said, "This'll get you on the bus with a
little left over."

Hoot looked surprised. He grabbed the money eagerly
and said, "You jus' givin' it to me fo' nothin'?"

"Yes. To help you get away from Creedy. But you better
get outa here. Jabbo's with us."

Hoot's eyes flashed with fear again at the mention of
Jabbo. As he glanced nervously toward the door, he said to
Jared, "I sho' 'preciate you doin' this, I sho' do. I won't
fo'get you fo' it."

Cy said, "I better look outside an' see if it's clear." He walked to the door and glanced down the street, then he came back inside quickly and said, "Jabbo's comin' down the sidewalk right now! You better get under the counter quick an' hide there 'til we're gone."

Hoot ran behind the counter as Cy hurriedly purchased two beers. He motioned for Jared to take a seat at an empty table. Just as they sat down, Jabbo entered. He walked over to them and said, "Mistuh Creedy didn't say fo' you to come into town to drink. You supposed to be lookin' fo' Hoot, not drinkin' beer."

"We done looked ev'rywhere," Cy said calmly, "an' we ain't seen hide or hair o' him. We thought we'd have a beer befo' goin' back to the bus. You want one?"

Jabbo stared at Cy. "You mean you goin' pay fo' it?" he questioned.

"That's what I said, ain't it?" Cy snapped. "You want one or not?"

Jabbo hesitated for a moment, and then he said, "I guess I'll have one. Then we got to go." He took a seat at the table while Cy went back to the counter.

Cy came back and handed Jabbo a bottle of beer. Jabbo took a drink and then said, "Mistuh Creedy goin' be maddern hell 'cause we didn't find that nigger."

"We looked ev'rywhere, but we didn't see nothin' at all of him," Cy said.

Jabbo's face became worried. "Maybe Mistuh Creedy find him in Belle Glade," he said.

"Maybe he will an' maybe he won't," Cy said. "If Hoot caught a ride on a truck, he could 'a shirt-tailed it halfway to Orlanda by now."

Cy took another drink, then he looked across the table and said, "Jabbo, how much Creedy payin' you to do what you doin' to yo' own folks? You a nigger too if you don't know it, just like me an' just like old Rude an' just like Hoot.

How much he payin' you?"

Jabbo ignored Cy's question. He turned up the bottle of beer, drained it, belched twice and said, "We better go now. We got to get back to the camp. Mistuh Creedy goin' be maddern hell."

The three of them walked back to the bus in silence. When they reached the camp, Jared and Cy went into the cabin and built a fire in the bucket; then they sat on the floor, eating a can of corned beef and drinking the rest of the wine.

Jared became thoughtful for several minutes, eating in silence. Then he turned to Cy and said, "How come them people back there in the cafe got so mad at me? I didn't do nothin' at all to make them mad."

"How come you so mad at Creedy?"

Cy's remark puzzled Jared. He said, "What you mean by that? I don't see that Creedy has anything to do with it."

Cy stopped eating and looked directly at Jared. "Did you see much diff'rence 'tween them nigger' quarters an' Angel City? Them folks back there works in the fields ev'ry day an' has to come back to them quarters ev'ry night. They can't get away no more than you can."

"You mean they think I'm to blame for it?" Jared asked, still puzzled.

"They don't think nothin'. They's just mad, just like you, mad 'cause they's trapped an' can't get out."

Jared became silent again for several moments, and then he muttered, "Well damn!"

They finished the can of corned beef as the small fire died down in the bucket. When the wine was gone, Jared lay down and wrapped himself in the blanket. For a long time he thought of what had happened in the cafe and why Cy said it happened. Although he was very tired, he felt restless. He turned to Cy and said, "You asleep?"

Cy grunted, "I was, but I ain't now."

"How come Creedy calls the camp Angel City?" Jared asked.

"I don't know," Cy answered, his voice reflecting a disinterest in further conversation. "Maybe he thinks it's the end o' the line fo' ev'rybody."

"Well, one angel flew the coop tonight, didn't he?"

Cy chuckled. "He sho' did. That's the God's truth."

Again Jared became silent for a moment, and then he said, "When my Papa died, they brung him into the house in a coffin, and then they opened it . . . I was sittin' there alone in that cold room, lookin' at him and feelin' sorrow fer Papa . . . and then all of a sudden I wasn't seein' Papa in that box at all . . . I was seein' me . . . me myself, right there in that pine box . . . not Papa in the coffin but me . . . and then I was alone in a city of angels, just like the Bible says . . . with nothin' around me but white forms . . . white forms driftin' all about me, speakin' in tongues I couldn't understand. . . . It was so real it like to have scared the life outen me, and it was a year or two afore I stopped seein' myself in that coffin . . . and that's the same way I've felt ever since I come to Angel City . . . like as if I'm just sittin' there lookin' at myself in a coffin, and there ain't no way out of it. I got a real bad feelin' in my gut, a mountain-bad feelin', and that's the worst kind."

Jared got up, gathered a few twigs from a pile in the corner and put them onto the coals in the bucket. After rolling himself back into the blanket, he said, "When we first come down here, all Kristy wanted was a red bathin' suit to wear to the beach, and all Bennie wanted was to see the ocean and fish in it. We been in Floridy all this time now and we ain't seen the ocean yet. I don't even know if it's really out there sommer or not."

"It's out there," Cy said. "But why don't you shut up now an' let me get some sleep? I'm bone tired, an' we got tomorrow to face. You ain't in no coffin yet."

Jared lay still for a long while, thinking again of the trip into Pahokee and the incident in the cafe and of Hoot escaping and of the things Cy had said to him. It was late in the night when he heard Creedy somewhere out in the darkness. Creedy was screaming wildly and shouting obscenities at Jabbo. Jared listened for several minutes, then he pulled the blanket over his head and went to sleep.

NINETEEN

ON MONDAY morning, the workers went back into the corn fields. The cold front had now passed, and Jared had spent most of Sunday afternoon bathing and washing his clothes in a drainage canal close by the camp. Later, he huddled in a blanket while the clothes dried slowly beside the small fire in the bucket.

Creedy was still in a rage over not finding Hoot, and each time Jared and Cy looked at his red face, they laughed inwardly because of the part they had played in Hoot's escape. By now he would be safely in Frostproof or Avon Park, and they knew that Hoot would never again come close to Homestead or to Belle Glade.

At mid-week they were shifted into a celery field, where they ripped the white stalks from the soot-black soil and threw them into dump trucks. The stalks were then hauled to the packing house in Belle Glade where they were dumped into vats of water, washed and cooled, packed into crates and shipped to distant supermarkets where they would be purchased, chopped into soups or salads or stuffed with pimiento cheese and served with hors d'oeuvres at cocktail parties.

Jared was thinking more and more of Cloma. Sometimes he worked an entire row without realizing it, and at times he threw the stalks of celery over the top of the truck and had to run back and pick them up. But Creedy made no mention, or showed any inclination of returning the crew to Angel City.

On Saturday afternoon, Creedy gave each of the men five dollars. They were waiting to board the bus for a trip to the country store when the pickup came down the dirt trail and stopped beside the Mark IV. A man got out of the truck and came over to Creedy.

Creedy glanced at the sign on the door of the pickup: *Okeechobee Produce Corporation.* The man looked around for a moment, studying the workers and the cabins. He then said to Creedy, "I was told somebody had moved into this camp. Are these your men?"

"I'm the contractor," Creedy replied cautiously.

"How long you been here?" the man asked.

"About a week and a half. How come you want to know?"

The man glanced around again and said, "This camp was condemned over five years ago. Who told you you could move in here?"

"Nobody," Creedy said, shuffling his feet. "I didn't think nobody would mind."

"This is company property, and you could get us in trouble with the health department. You'll have to move these people out of here."

"We ain't hurtin' nobody," Creedy said sullenly.

"We've got room for these men in a new camp east of Belle Glade. You can move them there right now. I'll radio ahead that you're coming."

"How much is it going to cost?" Creedy asked.

"The rent is ten dollars a man per week, but it's a new

building with baths, kitchens, heat and air conditioning. How many men you got here?"

Creedy didn't respond to the question. His face flushed as he said angrily, "I ain't payin' no ten dollars a week just for rent! You must think I'm crazy. That would run me around five hundred dollars just for a place for them to sleep."

"It won't cost you anything. It's taken out of each man's earnings, and they don't have to pay anything in advance."

"I ain't goin' to do it!" Creedy exploded. "I get the money and I pay the workers! They all owe me money, and I have to take it from their wages!"

The man stepped back and watched Creedy's face turn redder and redder. He said, "Listen, fellow! I'm not trying to tell you what to do with these men. That's between you and them. I'm just trying to help. But I'll tell you one thing for certain. You're going to move out of this camp. If you don't, I'll have the law out here."

Creedy calmed himself when he heard the law mentioned. He said in a more cooperative tone, "I don't mean to cause trouble. I just didn't think nobody would mind if we stayed here. We didn't mean no harm."

"You ought to know better than to come into an abandoned camp without permission!" the man snapped.

Creedy shuffled his feet again. "Can we stay here just for tonight and move in the morning?"

"I'm not saying that you can or can't. But at eight tomorrow morning I'm sending a deputy sheriff out here to check this property, and you better be to hell and gone out of here by then. You understand what I mean?"

"I understand," Creedy said, subdued.

The pickup was not out of sight down the dirt trail when Creedy kicked the rear tire of the bus violently and bellowed, "Goddamit to hell! A man can't even make a honest livin' no more!"

He had a lengthy conversation with Jabbo, then he got

into the Mark IV and screeched the tires down the dirt path. The trip to the store was cancelled.

At daylight the next morning the men were loaded into the bus. Creedy did not come back to the camp, and there was no box of canned food for breakfast. Jared shared the last of his corned beef with Cy, but most of the men had nothing.

The bus traveled back to Belle Glade and then to South Bay, but it didn't turn down Highway 27 toward Homestead. Instead, it continued west to Clewiston and out Highway 80 to LaBelle, where it turned south on Highway 29. Just after mid-morning, the old vehicle rolled into Immokalee.

Jabbo parked beside a service station on the highway leading through the main part of the town. Except for an occasional car or cattle truck ambling along, the streets were deserted. In the distance a church bell was tolling.

Jared gave Cy a questioning look, but Cy just shook his head in bewilderment. Jared had been in high spirits that morning, thinking that they were at last heading back to Angel City; but as they passed the junction of the highway to Homestead, and continued mile after mile into strange country, he became more and more puzzled and concerned.

It was two hours later when the Mark IV pulled in and parked beside the bus. Jabbo got out and went over to the car, and in a few minutes he came back, cranked the bus and followed Creedy through the town and south on Highway 29.

Seven miles past Immokalee the Mark IV turned left off the highway and followed a dirt path leading across a cow pasture. After a half mile they entered an area of dense lob-lolly pines, and then they came to an open field. Jabbo parked the bus and all of the men got out.

Creedy came over to the workers and said impatiently, "We got three hundred acres of cucumbers here to pick. I've contracted for the whole field 'stead of by the hamper. You men can sit on your butts the rest of the afternoon if you want to, but the sooner you get this field picked, the quicker we'll get out of here and head back to Homestead." He opened the car trunk and removed a box of canned food and a keg of water, then he got into the car and drove swiftly back across the pasture.

Some of the men took their blankets from the bus and started making a camp beneath a thick clump of pines. Others sat on the ground beside the bus.

Along a barbed wire fence separating the pasture from the field there were several stacks of empty hampers. Jared walked to the fence and picked up one of the hampers, then he went into the field alone and started picking.

TWENTY

IT WAS at two o'clock on Monday afternoon when Cloma felt the first sharp pain sear her stomach. She was sitting on an empty bean hamper outside the room, watching pickers in a field across the highway. She went into the room and sat on the edge of the bunk.

Another pain came in about fifteen minutes, this one more severe than the first. She lay down on the bunk, hoping that nothing more would happen. Then another came.

Cloma got up slowly and walked around the side of the building. The cook, sitting beneath a tree to the right of the trailer, did not look up as she approached. She watched the old man as he scratched idly in the dirt, and then she said, "I might need help before the others come back. I'm havin' pains."

The old man looked up blankly and said, "I's de cook. I don' pick no 'maters no mo', an' I gets two bottles o' wine 'stead o' one."

Cloma stared at him for a moment, then she said, "Don't you understand? I'm havin' pains! I might need help!"

He looked downward and started scratching in the dirt again. "I's de cook. I don' pick no 'maters no. . . ."

Cloma turned and walked away before he could finish. She went back to the room and sat on the bunk.

For an hour she sat still, flinching each time the pains came. She knew that she must not panic, and that there would be no one to help her until the workers came in from the fields.

Sweat beads formed on her forehead as time passed slowly, and her hands began to tremble. She concentrated as hard as she could and tried to close her mind to the pain. She thought of Jared, and wondered where he was and if he was all right. Then she drifted back to a time when she was a little girl, helping her mother make jelly from wild fox grapes her father picked in the woods behind their house. The smell of hot biscuits and fried chicken and baked ham drifted through the dim concrete room. She remembered a Christmas when a small porcelain doll had been left for her under a tree beside the fireplace; then her thoughts drifted to the day when she graduated from the sixth grade, and of the white dress her mother made for her, and the yellow ribbon her father bought for her to wear in her hair; and of how she was chosen to recite a poem by Lord Byron, and the piano music and the people in their Sunday suits and the two American flags in stands on each side of the stage; and in the summers there were fruits and vegetables to preserve for the winter, and games to play, and long Sunday afternoons spent exploring the woods and swimming in the creek. She then remembered the day she first noticed Jared, and how lanky and awkward he looked as he bid for her box of fried chicken at the church social, and how tenderly he brushed her shoulder as they walked to a picnic table to share the food, and how shy he was until they became one and shared their lives together; and how afraid he was when Kristy and Bennie were born; and the anger and fear and then sorrow when he lost the farm. Memories flashed through her mind like patterns in a kaleidoscope as she tossed and turned on the bunk. Several times she cried out, "Jared! Jared! My bed!"

Bennie came into the room just as his mother screamed. His face turned ashen, and for a moment he couldn't move. Then he raced around the west end of the barracks, shouting as he ran, "Miz Bertha! Miz Bertha!"

The Negro woman was about sixty years old. She was just over five feet tall and weighed nearly two hundred pounds, and she waddled like a goose as she walked. Her head was wrapped in a red bandana. As she came around the end of the building she was shouting, "Move outen de way! Move outen de way!" There was no one in front of her.

Bennie put a bucket of water on the cookshed grille and then stood outside the closed door of the room. Each time he heard his mother scream, he felt his stomach turn over and come into his throat. He ran back constantly to see if the water was hot, and when finally it was bubbling, he took it to the room. The woman met him at the door and said, "Now you stay outen here!"

Word spread rapidly through the camp what was happening. After supper, people began drifting to the room, attracted to birth just as people are attracted to death. It was not long before every person in the camp was sitting on the ground outside the door.

Bertha came outside once and was met by the unexpected audience. She said loudly, "You folks git on away from here! Dis ain't no circus! Ain't you never seen a baby borned befo'?" Still the people did not leave.

It was just past eight when the sound of a baby crying came from the room. Bennie wiped sweat from his face as Bertha came outside and announced triumphantly, "It's a boy! A fine baby boy!" She grinned broadly, then she went back into the room.

All of the people got up and left, and in a few minutes

they returned. Some were carrying cans of sardines and some beans and some Vienna sausage and some pickled pigs' feet and some slices of stale bread and some brought half-eaten pieces of hoop cheese. One by one they came to the door and placed the food on the floor just inside the room, then they disappeared again into the darkness.

Cloma looked through hazy eyes at the gifts. She said to Bertha, "They shouldn't have brought those things. They don't have food enough for themselves."

Bertha said, "They wants to, Miz Cloma. They's good folk."

Bertha continued sitting by the bunk, bathing Cloma's face with wet rags. Bennie darted in and out of the room, asking constantly, "Is my Mamma all right?"

Each time Bertha would answer in a commanding voice, "Yo' Mamma's fine! Now you git outen here! Dis ain't no place fo' a boy!"

About ten o'clock, Cloma sat up for a few minutes and held the baby. Bertha fed Cloma a few bites of Vienna sausage and said, "Yo' man sho' goin' be proud o' you. Dis a fine baby. What you goin' call him?"

"I don't know," Cloma answered. "It'll be up to Jared when he returns."

At midnight, Bennie came into the room and lay on his bunk. Although Bertha had to be in the fields at dawn, she continued sitting by the bunk, watching Cloma and the baby. She was still there when the bell rang for the bus to be loaded.

TWENTY-ONE

THE LAST of the cucumbers were picked at mid-morning Wednesday. The men gathered up their blankets from beneath the pine trees and boarded the bus, then the old vehicle crossed the dirt trail through the cow pasture and turned south on Highway 29.

At Carnestown they intersected with the Tamiami Trail and turned eastward into the Everglades. This change of scenery, so different from the rocky soil of Homestead or the black muck of Belle Glade, occupied Jared's attention for a time. He gazed out of the window and watched in fascination as they passed the clusters of Seminole and Miccosukee chickees scattered along the canals that flanked the highway; and the women in long colorful dresses, the souvenir stands and the air-boat riders; and then the vast open spaces of saw-grass broken in the distance by hammocks of somber cabbage palms.

When they came back to Highway 27 and turned south, Jared began to see things familiar to him: the drab brown rocky soil, the lines of Australian pines bordering drainage

canals, the fruit and vegetable stands at each intersection, the
farm roads that looked like strips of black ribbons as they
met the horizon, and the swarms of pickers following trucks
and tractors across fields. As his memory of all these things
came back to reality, it seemed to him that he had been gone
from Angel City for decades.

With each turn of the wheels, Jared thought more and
more of Cloma. He knew her time must have either come or
was very near. When they approached the outskirts of Homestead, he wanted to get out and push the old bus faster. Cy
noticed his extreme anxiety and said to him jokingly, "I
never thought I'd see you wantin' so bad to get back to
Angel City."

"I never thought I would," Jared replied, as he pictured
the camp in his mind.

He again stared out of the window as they passed the
small stucco building that housed the Homestead branch of
the sheriff's department; then they ambled through Florida
City and turned onto the highway leading to the camp.

Jared stood up in the bus when it reached the dirt road
leading through the tomato field. He moved to the front as
Jabbo got out and unlocked the gate, then he jumped from
the bus and ran quickly toward the barracks.

The camp was deserted, but Jared didn't notice this or
anything else. He found Cloma alone in the room, lying on
the bunk, the baby at her side. She sat up quickly when he
entered. For a moment they just looked at each other in
silence, then Jared dropped to his knees beside the bunk. He
touched her tenderly, and then his hand brushed against the
baby. He said, "Cloma, Cloma, I didn't want it to be this
way! I didn't want the baby born here. I thought we would
have our own place by now. I'm sorry, Cloma, I'm truly
sorry!"

As he leaned against her, she put her arm around his
shoulders and said softly, "It's all right, Jared. The baby's

fine, and that's all that matters. It's a boy."

He looked up when she said this. "A boy?"

"Yes. A boy."

He touched the baby again. "A boy," he repeated.

"What'll we name him?"

First he looked at her again, then he gazed at the baby. For a moment he drifted into deep thought, and then he said, "We'll call him Cy."

She smiled. "That's a fine name. Cy Teeter. That's a fine name for a boy."

He leaned over and kissed her, then he got up to leave the room. Cloma suddenly became serious and said, "Jared, you best see to Kristy as soon as you can. All she ever does now when she comes here is sit in a corner and sulk. Sometimes she holds her stomach and cries for a long time, and she hasn't said a dozen words to me since you been gone. I'm afraid they've done somethin' real bad to her, Jared. You best see to her soon as you can."

Jared was so elated by the birth of the baby that Cloma's concern for Kristy did not come through to him. He said hurriedly, "I'll see to it, Cloma. Don't you worry none. You just look after the boy." Then he turned quickly and passed through the door.

Cy was coming around the end of the building as Jared came from the room. Jared ran to him. "The baby's born!" he said, grabbing Cy's shoulders. "It's a boy! They're both fine, Cy! They're fine!"

Cy grinned. "A boy? Sho' nuff? A baby boy. That's good. I'm real proud fo' you."

Jared said, "We've named him Cy, after you."

Surprise flashed into Cy's eyes. He said, "Mistuh Jay, you sho' you want to name yo' boy after a nigger?"

"No," Jared said quickly, shaking his head. "I don't want to name him after a nigger. I want to name him after a friend. I want you to be his godfather."

Cy looked puzzled. He scratched his head and said, "Well, I ain't never been no godfather. What I have to do?"

"You don't have to do nothin'. You already done it."

Cy smiled. "Mistuh Jay, I'd be right pleased fo' that boy to be called Cy." He scratched his head again. "Cy Teeter. But I ain't never been no godfather."

Jared laughed. "You'll do fine. Now, don't you want to see your godson?"

"I sho' do!"

They both went into the room. Cy looked down and said, "That sho' be's a fine baby, Miz Cloma."

She looked up and smiled.

"A godfather," Cy said again. "Now ain't that somethin'. Me a godfather!"

Jared was smiling too.

TWENTY-TWO

JARED WENT back into the tomato fields the next day, but it would have made no difference to him if he were picking tomatoes or beans or corn or celery or cucumbers or cutting sugar cane. His thoughts were only on Cloma and the baby. He knew he must now get them out of Angel City, that it was beyond reason for the boy to either survive or grow up in such a place and under such conditions, but he also knew he must not do anything to endanger Kristy. He would not even think of risking one life for another. Although he constantly searched his mind for every possible avenue of escape, his answers came up blank.

Late that afternoon, Jared sat on the ground outside the room, still totally preoccupied with his thoughts of leaving Angel City. Cy was drinking the wine Jabbo had given him before supper. Jared turned to him and said, "You think Creedy might let us go now that the baby has come?"

Cy put down the bottle. "You know better'n that."

"We've got to get out of here. There must be a way."

"Don't you fool aroun' an' get yo'self in bad trouble

again," Cy said. "You got that baby to look out for now."

"That's why we've got to leave here now," Jared insisted. Then he got up suddenly. "I'll go and ask Creedy." Cy shook his head in dismay as he watched Jared go around the side of the building.

Creedy was standing by the trailer, talking to Jabbo. Jared walked up, stopped directly in front of Creedy and said abruptly, "Why don't you let us go now?"

The question caught Creedy by surprise. He said, "How come?"

"This ain't no fit place for a baby, and you know that as well as I do."

"What's wrong with it? I've seen nigger women pickin' in the fields with babies strapped to their backs. What's so diff'rent about your woman?"

Jared wanted to lash out and strike Creedy with his fists, but he controlled the anger and said, "I've been pickin' fer you fer a long time, and I know I've more than paid off the debt several times over. Why don't you let us go now?"

"Ain't nobody leaving Angel City owing me money!" Creedy exploded. "Nobody! You ought to know that by now! I ain't got time to listen no more! I'm busy!"

Jared glared harshly at Creedy, then he turned and went back to the barracks. He dropped down beside Cy and said, "What kind of a man is Creedy? Where'd he come from?"

"Most likely he was hatched in a buzzard's nest." Cy looked at the anger in Jared's eyes, knowing how the foolish quest with Creedy had ended. He said, "I done tole you befo'. The woods is full o' men like Creedy. He's scratchin' fo' ev'rything he can get, an' he don't care how he gets it. He done gone so far he couldn't turn back if he wanted to. He used to do this just to us niggers, but now he don't care who it is. You best stay clear o' him. He ain't human no more. He's daid too, just like all these folks in here he's done knocked the life out of."

"They's some good in ev'ry man," Jared said. "The Lord tells us so."

"The Lord ain't never lived in no migrant camp," Cy said. "Creedy ain't human no more. You best stay clear o' him."

For the rest of the week, Jared tried to brush the anger from his mind. He thought of many things other than Creedy and Angel City and the apparent hopelessness of his situation. He also spent more time after work with Cloma and the baby, and he didn't mention escape to Cy again.

On Sunday afternoon, Creedy brought all the children to the camp for the regular weekly visit. The next Tuesday would be Christmas Day, and Creedy had decided to leave them in the camp until Tuesday afternoon and avoid the expense of his housekeeper cooking them a Christmas dinner. Jared was thankful that Kristy would be with them for a few days, giving him a chance to try and find out what was bothering her so badly and perhaps bring her out of her deep depression. When Cloma first told him about Kristy's change, he did not listen, but what she had said gradually came through to him. He hoped that the change was simply because she was separated from the family.

The buses left for the fields as usual Monday morning, and a clear dawn was breaking as Jared started down the tomato row. He had decided to use Christmas as a tool to bring joy back to Kristy and make her her old self again, and he was sure this would work. He wanted to do something good for her and for everyone, and he was consumed with the same excitement he had always known on Christmas Eve. Cy watched him suspiciously when he started humming as he worked.

When the bus stopped at the store that afternoon, Jared made purchases other than the necessary food. He wanted to buy a red bathing suit for Kristy, but the store did not stock such items. Instead, he bought large bottles of cologne for Kristy and Cloma, a straw cowboy hat for Bennie, and knitted blue shoes for the baby. For Cy he selected a shaving mug, for Cy's son a toy bugle, and for Bertha a yellow cloth bonnet. He also bought a roll of pink ribbon, a package of red crepe paper, three boxes of paper cups, a basket of apples, a carton of eggs, and two pounds of bacon.

When he came into the room and Cloma saw all of these things, she knew that he must have spent the last of their savings, but she said nothing. This was the first time since they arrived in Angel City that she had seen happiness in his face, and she wanted to share this with him. She cut the sacks into pieces and wrapped each gift in brown paper, then she tied them with pieces of pink ribbon. Jared took the gift for Cloma out to the cookshed and wrapped it himself.

After supper, Jared did things that puzzled all of them. He brought three empty bean hampers from behind the cookshed and placed them together like a flat-topped Christmas tree; then he wrapped them with red crepe paper. Next, he brought the washtub from beside the hydrant and placed it on top of the hampers. On another hamper he sat the basket of apples.

Inside the room, lined against the walls, there were sixty-eight bottles of wine. With Bennie helping, all of the bottles were taken outside and emptied into the tub.

When all of this was finished, Jared asked Bennie and Kristy to go with him to the hampers. Bennie was puzzled but excited and eager, but Kristy turned back toward the room. Jared stepped in front of her and said, "It's Christmas Eve, Kristy. We're goin' to have a party just like we've always had."

For a moment Kristy remained silent, and then she said slowly, "It would be Christmas . . . in West Virginny . . . but there's no Christmas here."

"That's not so, Kristy," Jared said gently. "It's Christmas

ev'rywhere. God isn't just in West Virginny. We'll have a fine party . . . it's Christmas ev'rywhere." He reached out and gripped her hand tightly.

Cloma held the baby on a hamper outside the room and watched as Jared led Kristy out to the decorated hampers with Bennie following. Jared started to sing, "Silent Night . . . Holy Night . . . All is calm . . . All is bright. . . ." Bennie joined in immediately, but Kristy remained silent.

People came out of the rooms and peered curiously at the strange gathering. One by one, and then in groups, they gradually drifted forward, forming a circle around the hampers and blending their voices into the singing of the carols. Soon all the camp was there. Jared marveled at the perfect blending of the rich Negro voices. He had never heard Christmas music sung so beautifully.

Kristy did not join in the singing, but she suddenly looked up and said, "Don't you worry none about me, Papa. I'm not fittin' to cause you worry. I'm sorry, Papa, I don't mean to be a bother to you." Jared tightened his grip on her hand.

After several more carols, paper cups were dipped into the tub of wine. The apples would be given out and eaten later. Soon again the camp and the surrounding fields were ringing with the sounds of Christmas.

Once Jared looked over and noticed Jabbo and Clug standing beneath the floodlight on the east end of the building, watching. He walked over to them and said, "Why don't you join us? It's Christmas Eve."

They both looked perplexed. Jabbo said, "Mistuh Creedy didn't say nothin' 'bout no singin'."

"Creedy's not here tonight," Jared said. "You can join us if you want to. It's up to you."

For a moment they seemed hesitant, but as Jared walked back to the circle, Jabbo and Clug turned and disappeared in the direction of the trailer.

No one wanted the music to stop. It was after midnight when the camp again became silent, and the people drifted slowly back to their rooms.

TWENTY-THREE

ON CHRISTMAS morning, Jared asked Cy and his son and Bertha to join them. While the gifts were being opened, Jared fixed everyone a breakfast of the eggs and bacon. All of them felt a tinge of guilt as the odor of frying bacon drifted throughout the camp. Others were having sardines and Vienna sausage.

It was shortly after noon when Creedy came to the camp. Jared and Cy were sitting on the ground outside the room when Jabbo and Clug approached. Jabbo stopped in front of Jared and said, "Mistuh Creedy say the girl stay here now an' work in the fields. He want the baby."

"What?" Jared said, springing to his feet. "What'd you say?"

Jabbo repeated, "Mistuh Creedy say he want the baby. He's done with the girl, an' you can have her back now. He say she's tetched, an' she ain't much of a woman noways. She don't know how to take a man. I tried 'er myself when Mistuh Creedy was gone."

Jared lunged furiously at the giant black man as Cy

jumped up and ran into his room. Jabbo whipped a pistol from his belt and smashed it into Jared's face. The blow spun him backward against the wall. For a moment he stared at Jabbo, then he slumped to the ground.

Cy came out of the room holding a butcher knife. He stepped in front of Jabbo and said, "You tetch that baby it goin' be the last thing you ever tetch! You understand me, black nigger?" He pointed the knife at Jabbo's throat.

Jabbo looked at the long blade as he stepped back and said, "We goin' take the baby. You want to get yo'self killed fo' it?"

Cy went into a crouching position. He said, "You'll have to kill me right here in the camp! It won't be out in the swamp where nobody can see! You'll have to do it right here in front of ev'rybody!"

Jabbo pointed the pistol at Cy and said, "You go with us to see Mistuh Creedy. You don't go, I'll blow yo' guts all over the ground."

Cy straightened up to a standing position. He gripped the knife handle harder and said, "I'll go see Creedy, but you ain't tetchin' that baby. You'll have to kill me first."

Jared pushed himself up and saw Cy walking with Jabbo and Clug around the side of the building. Cloma, Kristy and Bennie rushed from the room, and all of them had stark terror in their faces. Jared motioned frantically for them to go back inside, then he staggered along the wall and out to the cookshed.

Hanging on a rafter in the shed there was a large steel hook the cook used to remove pots from the grille. Jared took it down and made his way slowly along the south fence. When he passed the end of the building he could see Cy standing in front of Creedy, with Jabbo and Clug behind him. They were arguing violently. Creedy also had a pistol in his hand. Jabbo and Clug suddenly grabbed Cy and started dragging him toward the pickup. He broke free and came at

Creedy with the knife. Jared watched as Creedy fired point blank; then Cy slumped to the ground. Jabbo and Clug picked him up and threw him into the back of the pickup.

Sweat was pouring from Jared's face as he crept closer, coming in behind the trailer so they couldn't see him. He eased around the side of the trailer and was just to the side of Creedy when Creedy turned. Disbelief flashed into Creedy's eyes as the steel hook smashed into the center of his head. He stared blankly for a moment, then he toppled backward. The pistol fell at Jared's feet.

The bullet stung like a wasp when it hit Jared's left shoulder. He grabbed Creedy's pistol and looked up. Jabbo was about to fire at him again. He pointed quickly and pulled the trigger, and the bullet caught Jabbo in the right arm. Jabbo dropped the pistol and stepped back.

For a moment Jared couldn't move, and he felt hot blood running down the inside of his shirt. He finally pushed himself up and walked to Jabbo and Clug.

Clug looked at the pistol in the trembling hand and at the anger in Jared's eyes. He took a step backward and said wildly, "I didn't mean no harm! I swear fo' God I didn't! Mistuh Creedy made me do it!"

Jabbo remained silent, also watching Jared's trembling hand.

Jared turned to Jabbo and said, "Jabbo, I ought to kill you right now! You ain't fitten to live, the things you've did." He pointed the pistol directly at the giant black man's head, and then he hesitated, as if trying to make a decision. He finally lowered the gun and said, "I'll tell you what I want. I want both of you to walk down to the gate and step outside. Then I want you to run. And I don't want you to stop or look back 'til you reach Homestead. You understand me?"

Clug nodded his head in agreement, but Jabbo stood still and said, "You must be crazy, white man!"

Jared aimed the pistol and fired. The bullet knocked a

piece of leather from Jabbo's right shoe. He jumped back quickly and then he followed Clug to the gate. Jared watched as the two men ran down the dirt road toward the highway.

Bennie came around the corner of the building and ran to his father. He said wildly, "Are you hurt, Papa? Are you hurt?"

Jared shook Bennie's shoulder to calm him, then he said, "I want you to run to the store and get them to call Deputy Drummond at the sheriff's department. Tell him to come out here real quick and send an ambulance, that they's people hurt out here. You'll have to run faster than you've ever run before. Can you do this, Bennie?"

"I can do it, Papa," Bennie said. "It won't take me no time at all to get to the store." He bounded across the clearing and out the gate, then he cut at an angle across the tomato field toward the highway.

Jared's head was beginning to pound, but he paid no heed to this or to the severe pain in his shoulder. For a moment he watched after Bennie, then he walked back to where Creedy was lying on the ground. Creedy didn't move as Jared dropped down and straddled the huge hulk. He sat on Creedy's chest and pointed the pistol directly into Creedy's face. Jared's hand trembled harder as he pressed his finger against the trigger.

From behind him he heard a voice calling, "Mistuh Jay! Mistuh Jay!"

Cy was dragging himself across the ground. Jared was startled, for he thought they had killed Cy. The pistol barrel was still pressed against Creedy's face when Cy yelled, "Don't do it, Mistuh Jay! Don't do it! He ain't worth it! Let it be!"

For a moment Jared did not remove the pistol, then he suddenly remembered something Cy had once said to him, "... *you goin' end up doin' somethin' bad you would have never done.*" He threw the pistol to the ground and went over to Cy.

The front of Cy's shirt was soaked with blood. Jared bent over him and said, "How bad is it?"

Cy tried to manage a smile. "If I had a choice, I'd ruther not have it at all. But they ain't done me in yet. It's a hard job to kill a nigger."

Jared looked into his eyes and said, "When this's all over, Cy, let's do somethin' together. We'll be pardners in somethin'."

"That would sho' be fine," Cy said weakly. "But let's see if we can do somethin' 'sides pick 'maters."

Jared put his arms under Cy and picked him up. The weight of Cy's body sent sharp pains searing through his shoulder, yet he didn't waver as he walked slowly to the room and placed Cy on one of the bunks.

Kristy was sitting on a bunk against the opposite wall, clutching the rag doll that Jeff Billings had given her the night before they left West Virginia. Jared turned to her and said, "See to Cy as best you can, Kristy. Bennie has gone fer an ambulance."

Kristy didn't answer, and she seemed not to hear or see Jared. She pushed herself back against the wall and tightened her grip on the doll.

Jared said harshly, "Kristy! Don't you hear me? I want you to look after Cy!"

A wildness came into her eyes, and suddenly she jumped up and ran screaming from the room.

Jared stumbled outside and found Cloma sitting cross-legged on the ground, holding the baby. She was swaying back and forth, singing, "Jesus . . . loves me . . . this I know . . . for the . . . Bible . . . tells me so . . . little ones . . . to Him belong . . . they are weak . . . and He . . . is strong. . . ."

For a moment Jared stared at her blankly, as if seeing someone other than Cloma, and then he said, "Cloma . . . are you all right, Cloma?"

She looked up, but her eyes showed no recognition. She

said, "There's snow now in West Virginny. The school will be a long walk for the children." Then she started swaying again, swaying and singing, "Yes . . . Jesus loves me . . . yes . . . Jesus loves me . . . yes . . . Jesus loves me . . . the Bible tells . . . me so. . . ."

Jared dropped down beside her and said in anguish, "Oh my God! My God have mercy! What have I done to them? What have I done . . . ?"

For a moment more he watched her, trying to disbelieve what he was seeing, wanting to reach out and touch her and the baby, but not doing so; and then he was suddenly over-whelmed with rage. He jumped up and rushed around the east side of the building, totally unaware of the people huddled in groups along the wall, people watching with fear and bewilderment in their eyes. He climbed into the red bus and cranked it, then he backed it into the clearing. When he gave it full throttle, the old vehicle shuddered forward and crashed into the side of the trailer, sending it tumbling over on its side.

Jared then backed the bus again, turned it and aimed it full speed at the north fence. It rammed into the thick mesh wire and seemed to bounce back. The fence swayed for a moment, then it toppled to the ground.

Jared got out of the bus and walked trance-like to the pickup. His eyes were glazed, and the pounding in his head had become almost unbearable. He noticed that Creedy had dragged himself to a sitting position beside the Mark IV, but his eyes were still closed.

When Jared reached the pickup, he removed the gas cap and dropped a lighted match into the tank. The force of the explosion knocked him backward, and he crawled away as a mushroom of fire enveloped the truck.

Jared lay on the ground and watched without emotion as the flames consumed the pickup, then he pushed himself up and went out of the gate and into the tomato field. He pulled one of the plants from the ground and threw it into the air. Then he pulled another and another, throwing them wildly. He was still moving down the row, sailing plants into the air, when he heard the scream of a siren. The wailing sound brought him back to consciousness, and he turned and went back to the gate.

The patrol car was leading an ambulance, and Bennie was on the front seat with the deputy. Jared stepped aside as the two vehicles rushed past him and parked just inside the gate. White dust boiled into his face as he forced himself to the ambulance. He held on to the front fender and said, "My friend's down there in room ten. See to him first. He's been shot pretty bad." Then he felt darkness rush in as he toppled to the ground.

Jared was not aware again until he looked up into the face of one of the ambulance attendants. The deputy and Bennie were standing to one side. He asked, "How's my friend?"

"He took a good one," the attendant said, "but we think he'll make it."

"What about Creedy?"

"You mean the big one?"

"Yes. The big one. Is he dead?"

"Naw, he's o.k. His skull's probably cracked, but that's nothing new. We get plenty of those every day out of these camps. But you can bet he'll have some kind of a headache tomorrow. You folks sure had some donnybrook of a Christmas party out here."

The deputy leaned over Jared and said, "He'll have more than a headache for a long time to come. Your son has told me all the things you told me before, and now maybe some of these other people will talk. He's got a lot to answer for, including that bullet in your friend."

The words meant nothing to Jared. He was glad that he hadn't killed Creedy, but he no longer cared about him or

Angel City, and he received no satisfaction from the thought of what might happen to Creedy. He said absently, ". . . it don't matter none noway . . . the woods is full of 'em . . . ."

The deputy leaned over him again. "Don't worry about your family or any of these other people," he said. "I'm sending welfare workers out here to help them. They'll be o.k."

Bennie came to his father and said, "What we goin' to do when we leave here, Papa? I need to know what we'll do."

"I don't know, Bennie," Jared said weakly. "I just don't rightly know. Maybe that fruit stand is still out there sommers, and maybe we'll have to go back to the mountains so's I can work in the mines. We'll make it somehow, I promise you. But you got to take care of your Mamma and the baby and Kristy while I'm gone. You just got to do it, son. You hear?"

"I can do it, Papa," Bennie said. "Don't you worry none at all. I'll see to them."

Jared reached out and squeezed Bennie's hand as he felt himself being lifted into the ambulance. He said urgently, "Do your best by them, Bennie! They're goin' need all the help you can give."

As soon as the two flashing vehicles crossed the dirt road and turned onto the highway, some of the people trudged slowly back to their rooms. Others did not.

Several men went to the open gate and stepped out. For several minutes they stood still, looking back at the barracks and the flattened fence and the smoldering hulk of the pick-up. Then they moved forward hesitantly. Suddenly they started running, and soon there was a pounding of feet as they rushed across the tomato field toward the open highway.

If you enjoyed reading this book, here are some other books from Pineapple Press on related topics. To request a catalog or to place an order, visit our website at www.pineapplepress.com. Or write to Pineapple Press, P.O. Box 3889, Sarasota, Florida 34230, or call 1-800-PINEAPL (746-3275).

OTHER BOOKS BY PATRICK SMITH

A Land Remembered. In this best-selling novel, Patrick Smith tells the story of three generations of the MacIveys, a Florida family who battle the hardships of the frontier to rise from a dirt-poor Cracker life to the wealth and standing of real estate tycoons.

Forever Island. A classic novel of the Everglades, *Forever Island* tells the story of Charlie Jumper, a Seminole Indian who clings to the old ways and teaches them to his grandson, even as the white man's world encroaches upon his own.

Allapattah is the story of a young Seminole in despair in the white man's world. Toby Tiger refuses to bend to the white man's will and fights back the only way he knows how. The word allapattah is Seminole for crocodile, a creature that earns Toby's respect and protection.

The River Is Home. Smith's first novel revolves around a Mississippi family's struggle to cope with changes in their rural environment. Poor in material possessions, Skeeter's kinfolk are rich in their appreciation of their beautiful natural surroundings.

A Land Remembered, Student Edition. This best-selling novel is now available to young readers in two volumes. In this edition, the first chapter becomes the last so that the rest of the book is not a flashback. Some of the language and situations have been altered slightly for younger readers.

A Land Remembered Goes to School by Tillie Newhart and Mary Lee Powell. An elementary school teacher's manual, using *A Land*

Remembered to teach language arts, social studies, and science, coordinated with the Sunshine State Standards of the Florida Department of Education.

Middle School Teacher Plans and Resources for A Land Remembered: Student Edition by Margaret Paschal. The vocabulary lists, comprehension questions, and post-reading activities for each chapter in the student edition make this teacher's manual a valuable resource. The activities aid in teaching social studies, science, and language arts coordinated with the Sunshine State Standards.

CRACKER WESTERNS

Alligator Gold by Janet Post. On his way home at the end of the Civil War, Caleb Hawkins is focused on getting back to his Florida cattle ranch. But along the way, Hawk encounters a very pregnant Madelaine Wilkes and learns that his only son has gone missing and that his old nemesis, Snake Barber, has taken over his ranch.

Bridger's Run by Jon Wilson. Tom Bridger has come to Florida in 1885 to find his long-lost uncle and a hidden treasure. It all comes down to a boxing match between Tom and the Key West Slasher.

Riders of the Suwannee by Lee Gramling. Tate Barkley returns to 1870s Florida just in time to come to the aid of a young widow and her children as they fight to save their homestead from outlaws.

Ghosts of the Green Swamp by Lee Gramling. Saddle up your easy chair and kick back for a Cracker Western featuring that rough-and-ready but soft-hearted Florida cowboy, Tate Barkley, introduced in *Riders of the Suwannee*.

Guns of the Palmetto Plains by Rick Tonyan. As the Civil War explodes over Florida, Tree Hooker dodges Union soldiers and Florida outlaws to drive cattle to feed the starving Confederacy.

Thunder on the St. Johns by Lee Gramling. Riverboat gambler Chance Ramsay teams up with the family of young Josh Carpenter and the trapper's daughter Abby Macklin to combat a slew of greedy outlaws seeking to destroy the dreams of honest homesteaders.

Trail from St. Augustine by Lee Gramling. A young trapper, a crusty ex-sailor, and an indentured servant girl fleeing a cruel master join forces to cross the Florida wilderness in search of buried treasure and a new life.

Wiregrass Country by Herb and Muncy Chapman. Set in 1835, this historical novel will transport you to a time when Florida settlers were few and laws were scarce. Meet the Dovers, a family of homesteaders determined to survive against all odds and triumph against the daily struggles that accompany running a cattle ranch.

FLORIDA HISTORY

Old Florida Style: A Story of Cracker Cattle (DVD) by Steve Kidd and Alex Menendez, Delve Productions. This DVD showcases Florida's Cracker heritage. Saddle up a tough little Cracker horse called a marsh tacky and explore old Florida—when cow hunters pulled the rugged Spanish cattle out of the palmettos and established this as a cattle state.

Time Traveler's Guide to Florida by Jack Powell. A unique guidebook that describes 70 places and reenactments in Florida where you can experience the past, and a few where you can time-travel into the future.

Florida's Past: People and Events that Shaped the State by Gene Burnett. The three volumes in this series are chock-full of carefully researched, eclectic essays written in Gene Burnett's easygoing style. Many of these essays on Florida history were originally published in *Florida Trend* magazine.

Tropical Surge by Benjamin Reilly. This engaging historical narrative covers many significant events in the history of south Florida, including the major developments and setbacks in the early years of Miami and Key West, as well as an in-depth look at Henry Flagler's amazing Overseas Railway.

OTHER FICTION

Adventures in Nowhere by John Ames. A boy in 1950s Florida wrestles with adult problems and enjoys the last days of his boyhood in a place called Nowhere, sometimes fearing for his sanity as his family falls apart and he watches a house change shape across the river.

Seven Mile Bridge by Michael Biehl. Florida Keys dive shop owner Jonathan Bruckner returns home to Sheboygan, Wisconsin, after his mother's death. What he finds leads him to an understanding of the mystery that surrounded his father's death years before.

The Bucket Flower by Donald Robert Wilson. In 1893, 23-year-old Elizabeth Sprague goes into the Everglades to study its unique plant life, even though she's warned that a pampered "bucket flower" like her can't endure the rigors of the swamp. She encounters wild animals and even wilder men but finds her own strength and a new future.

My Brother Michael by Janis Owens. Out of the shotgun houses and deep, shaded porches of a West Florida mill town comes this extraordinary novel of love and redemption. Gabriel Catts recounts his lifelong love for his brother's wife, Myra—whose own demons threaten to overwhelm all three of them.

Black Creek by Paul Varnes. Through the story of one family, we learn how white settlers moved into the Florida territory, taking it from the natives—who had been there only a few generations—with false treaties and finally all-out war. Thus, both sides were newcomers anxious to "take Florida."

Confederate Money by Paul Varnes. In 1861, as this novel opens, a Confederate dollar is worth 90 cents. We follow Henry Fern as he fights on both sides of the war. Through shrewd dealings, he manages to amass $40,000 in Confederate paper money and finally changes his paper fortune into silver and gold.

For God, Gold and Glory by E. H. Haines. The riveting account of the invasion of the American Southeast from 1539 to 1543 by Hernando de Soto, as told by his private secretary, Rodrigo Ranjel. A meticulously researched tale of adventure and survival and the dark aspects of greed and power.

Nobody's Hero by Frank Laumer. Based on the true adventure of an American soldier who refused to die in spite of terrible wounds sustained during the battle known as Dade's Massacre, which started the Second Seminole War in Florida.

THE HONOR SERIES

"Sign on early and set sail with Peter Wake for both solid historical context and exciting sea stories." —U.S. Naval Institute Proceedings

The Honor Series of naval fiction by Robert N. Macomber. Covers the life and career of American naval officer Peter Wake from 1863 to 1907. The first book in the series, *At the Edge of Honor,* won Best Historical Novel from the Florida Historical Society. The second, *Point of Honor,* won the Cook Literary Award for Best Work in Southern Fiction. The sixth, *A Different Kind of Honor,* won the Boyd Literary Award for Excellence in Military Fiction from the American Library Association.